DEADLIER THAN THE FEMALE

When Teresa, the beautiful bargirl, asked Canyon up to her room, she also gave him a warning.

"Lance Caulder is up there, with his foreman, Karl Berdick," she said. "He told me to get you upstairs pronto."

"His gun is unholstered?" Canyon said.

"He is holding it at his side."

Canyon looked at Teresa. She had a damn pretty face. He knew what Caulder would do to it in revenge if Canyon cleared out.

He gave Teresa a long, slow smile. "I think it's time we went upstairs," he said.

CANYON O'GRADY RIDES ON

CANYON O'GRADY

15

DEATH
RANCH

by
Jon Sharpe

Ⱥ

A SIGNET BOOK

SIGNET
Published by the Penguin Group
Penguin Books USA Inc., 375 Hudson Street,
New York, New York 10014, U.S.A.
Penguin Books Ltd, 27 Wrights Lane,
London W8 5TZ, England
Penguin Books Australia Ltd, Ringwood,
Victoria, Australia
Penguin Books Canada Ltd, 10 Alcorn Avenue,
Toronto, Ontario, Canada M4V 3B2
Penguin Books (N.Z.) Ltd, 182–190 Wairau Road,
Auckland 10, New Zealand

Penguin Books Ltd, Registered Offices:
Harmondsworth, Middlesex, England

First published by Signet,
an imprint of New American Library,
a division of Penguin Books USA Inc.

First Printing, September, 1991
10 9 8 7 6 5 4 3 2 1

Canyon O'Grady

His was a heritage of blackguards and poets, fighters and lovers, men who could draw a pistol and bed a lass with the same ease.

Freedom was a cry seared into Canyon O'Grady, justice a banner of his heart.

With the great wave of those who fled to America, the new land of hope and heartbreak, solace and savagery, he came to ride the untamed wildness of the Old West.

With a smile or a six-gun, Canyon O'Grady became a name feared by some and welcomed by others, but remembered by all . . .

The New Mexico Territory, 1867,
where a murderous Confederate bushwhacker
has come to ground to spread his own
unique brand of terror and betrayal . . .

1

"Yes, yes, Mr. O'Grady," said the president, his powerful voice filling the room. "I know the war is over. And Quantrill is dead. But Lance Caulder is still alive and still capable of fomenting disorder. This notion of a Confederacy dies hard, it seems. But it is for his crimes that I want Caulder apprehended and brought to trial—just as those responsible for Andersonville are being brought to justice."

Canyon nodded, acutely aware of the beleaguered president's indignation and conviction. It had been storming in Washington for days now and the sound of the windswept raindrops rattling at the window panes filled the oval office with a melancholy sound.

"I need hardly remind you, Canyon, that this is not a happy time for me. This Republican Congress is doing what it can to cut me down, but this, at least, I can see to."

"I understand, sir," said Canyon.

As Canyon spoke, the president's aide, Colonel Charles Cutler, entered from an anteroom and paused a few feet inside the door. At his appearance, the president—a bent, gray-haired figure—

got up from behind his massive desk and walked over to the window. Ignoring the two men, he looked out at the rain for a moment, seemingly lost in thought, then squared his shoulders and turned to fix his gaze on Canyon.

"Yes, O'Grady. My mind is made up. It does not matter what this congress has in store for me. I want Caulder brought to justice." The president glanced at the colonel. "I'll leave the rest up to you, Charles."

With a brisk nod of dismissal, President Andrew Johnson waited for Canyon to follow the colonel into the the next room. As Canyon left the oval office, he saw Johnson once more at the window, his hands clasped behind his back as he gazed through the rain-streaked window, a lonely, stubborn veteran of the political wars who was now taking his share—and more than his share—of hard knocks for his efforts to bring this still-divided nation back together again the way Lincoln would have wanted it—with malice toward none and charity for all.

Once he was inside his office, Colonel Cutler closed the door and indicated with a thrust of his bearded chin a leather Morris chair sitting beside his desk. Canyon sat down in it as the colonel moved around behind his desk, slumped wearily into his swivel chair, and peered at Canyon for a long moment, his shrewd eyes appraising him carefully.

"This man Caulder," he began without preamble, "is alive and well in New Mexico, and from what I hear is still boasting of his infamous exploits in the war."

"Would that be the man who wiped out those Union prisoners at Cherry Cross Station?"

"That's the bastard, all right. Not a single Union prisoner was left alive, and after they were cut down, some of them had their genitals sliced off for good measure and stuffed into their mouths."

Canyon stirred uncomfortably in his chair. "I heard about that—the rumors, I mean."

"Unfortunately, O'Grady, they were not rumors. Of course, some have maintained that Caulder was only doing what Quantrill ordered, but he had broken with Quantrill by that time and he and his men were on their own."

"Do you know where in New Mexico he is?"

"Placer Town, in the mountains northwest of Santa Fe. As I understand, this was a Confederate nest during the war; its ranchers provided fresh meat for the Confederacy. It is still filled with Confederate sympathizers, I am afraid, and to most of them Lance Caulder is pretty much of a hero. You'll be riding into a scorpion's nest of unregenerated rebels, I am afraid."

"I'm grateful for the warning," Canyon said, smiling ruefully.

"But you won't be alone. There's a Secret Service agent already out there. A fine operative. He's the one found Caulder. Name's Barton. Seth Barton. He's been instructed to wait for your arrival before making any move on Caulder. How soon can you leave?"

"Tomorrow. The sooner I put this ugly weather behind me, the better. But I need to know more about Caulder and this town."

"Yes, yes, of course. I've already seen to that. At what hotel are you staying now?"

Canyon told him.

"Be in your suite tonight after eight. My aide will bring you your traveling funds as well as an extensive file on Lance Caulder and this town. Study the file, then return it to my aide. There's one thing more."

"What, Colonel?"

"If any of this comes out, the president will deny everything. For his own reasons, he does not want to appear to be holding a grudge against any of those who fought for the Confederacy—even scum like this bushwhacker."

"It won't get out, Colonel. Not from these lips, anyway."

"The president knows that, O'Grady. It's why he has called you in on this."

Canyon got to his feet. "I'll be waiting for that aide, Colonel."

"Good luck, Mr. O'Grady."

"Thank you, Colonel."

Canyon strode from the room.

The afternoon was half gone and the heat had reached a cruel intensity as Canyon rode north toward the dark peaks ahead. Nothing relieved the sun's pounding intensity. A hundred out here, he figured, maybe hotter—enough to curl a lizard's hide. The edges of his saddle were hot and the bridle's metal sent painful glints into his eyes. He raised his bandanna over his nose to keep the stinging dust out of his nostrils.

It was near five before he lifted from the baked

flat into rolling foothills. An occasional pine stood as lonely sentinels against the distant peaks still hanging tantalizingly before him, black and bulky and lofty. Before him, a narrow white trace coiled upward to vanish in the timber. He followed it across a shallow creek, pausing long enough to let his palomino satisfy its thirst, then kept on until he had lifted into the cool, shadowed benchlands, the timbered foothills so close now he could smell the pine's sharp tang.

He turned then and craned his neck to gaze back the way he had come. Yes, the rider was still in sight, as hard to catch with the eye as a flea on an old dog. Whether the rider was following Canyon or not was open to question. This was, after all, the only trace through these hills and Canyon did not have to be the only one with business in this part of the world.

Still, he considered it wise to keep an eye on the rider—just in case.

Turning back around, he urged his mount on, eager to lift into the distant timber's cool, green ranks. As the sun sank, his shadow stretched out farther and farther to his left. Reaching the foothills at last, he turned to see if he could catch another glimpse of the man behind him. But the rider had vanished, swallowed up by the vast, prowling shadows growing now along the benchland.

Canyon squinted into the sun's red glow, catching the last great burst of flame as it edged below the earth's rim. Instantly, the world was transformed into another place—blue and still, the air redolent with the tang of pine from the green-clad hills about him. A sweet coolness from the distant peaks flowed against him, taking a little of the curse off the day's relentless heat. Urging on the palomino, he kept riding toward the foothills, following the rutted trace that led between the timber-clad slopes.

It was well past dusk when he came to Placer Town. It sat upon a bench facing the foothills, a double row of buildings on either side of the main street with narrow side streets branching off it and more buildings scattered about in the semi-darkness on bare, timbered-off hills or perched atop wooded gullies. Beyond the town, the road kept on into a canyon until it vanished into the sheer, vertical land of towering peaks that reared into the sky above the town like ominous, titanic guardians.

He let the road carry him across a booming, wooden plank bridge and down the main street past single-story houses. Their lights bloomed through dusty windows, casting a fitful glow over the roadway ahead of him. At the center of town, another road cut out of the hills to form an intersection. Though this was New Mexico, there was no trace of Spanish influence, no town square fronted with low, stuccoed buildings, like Santa Fe. The architecture was oddly southern, as if in the midst of these dark, glowering peaks the townspeople were trying to create another Dixie.

On the four corners sat a hotel, a general store, and two saloons that faced each other across the wide intersection. One saloon, the smaller of the two, seemed to have no name; the other one, facing the hotel, was called The Owl Hoot, its sign freshly painted. Next to it was a livery stable, toward which Canyon guided his mount. An old man materialized out of the stable's gloom and peered up at Canyon.

"Third stall back," he said.

Canyon dismounted and gave the palomino a small drink at the street trough before leading it into the livery, where he removed his saddle and other gear. He snaked his Henry out of the scabbard, then draped the saddle over the partition separating the stalls. For a moment he stood there, his big gentle hand exploring the sweat-gummed back of the horse, checking it for blisters. Satisfied the palomino was free of them, he left the stall and walked out into the street, bent over the drinking trough's feed pipe and let the icy water roll into his throat and fill up his belly until it would hold no more. He straightened up and wiped off his mouth with the back of his hand and kept on into the smaller saloon, his saddle bags slung over one shoulder, his Henry in his right hand.

It was the supper hour and slack time. He leaned his rifle against the bar and stood there with no company except the barkeep. He took his whiskey neat and returned to the street, pausing on the porch to look over this small, grim town huddled under the shadowing peaks, aware of a current of cool air flowing out of the mountains.

The odor of food from the hotel restaurant across the street had an effect on him so immediate that a sharp pain started in the corners of his jaws. He saw townsmen moving idly in and out of the hotel, bound to and from supper. Others strolled past the saloon on the wooden walk, each one as he passed giving Canyon a quick, bold glance, making no effort to hide their curiosity. He was a stranger and every man in town knew it. And there was not one who did not glance with gleaming eyes at his well-oiled Henry.

Across the street, a tall man left the hotel and started to walk toward Canyon, his lanky body alternately clear, then dark as he passed through the lamplit beams shining from nearby windows. There was a sharp edge to his square shoulders. A flatbrimmed Stetson sat slightly forward on his head, keeping his eyes in shadow.

When he reached the wooden sidewalk in front of the saloon, he mounted the steps and paused alongside Canyon, glancing idly about as he did so. He had yellow hair and a light skin blistered almost raw from the sun. When he glanced at Canyon, his green eyes glinted in the light from the saloon.

"Are you O'Grady?" he asked, his lips barely moving.

Canyon nodded and moved out of the light into the darker portion of the saloon porch.

"I'm Seth Barton," the man told Canyon.

"You found Caulder, did you?"

"I found him, all right. But we'll have to go slow."

"Where is he?"

"Later. Eat your supper. I'll meet you in my hotel room later. Room 25. Third floor in back."

After glancing nervously about him, Barton left Canyon, strode back along the porch and shouldered through the batwings into the saloon. Canyon was about to cross the street to the hotel restaurant, when he saw the rider who had trailed him from Santa Fe ride past.

He was a short man with a heavy brush of a mustache and thick, tousled hair that came to his shoulders. Both he and his horse were as pale as ghosts from alkali dust. The rider did not flick a single glance in Canyon's direction, but there was no doubt in Canyon's mind that he had been spotted by the rider and his presence noted. In a moment, the ghostly rider had disappeared into the street's gloom farther on.

Canyon crossed the street to the hotel, signed the register, and climbed a set of squeaking stairs to a room on the second floor facing the main street. He dumped his Henry and the rest of his gear into a corner, then took off his coat and shirt and filled the washbowl from the pitcher. As soon as his big, rough hands applied the soap and water to his face, he felt the mask of alkali dust crumbling. Tough though his face was, the soap stung its scorched surface. It had sure as hell been a hot day.

Unwilling to wait until the next day to rid himself of the trail's grime, he stripped, revealing broad, powerful shoulders and lean shanks with not an extra ounce of tallow on his tightly muscled waist. The merciless sun and the cutting winds of the many trails he had followed in this rough, new land had cured his face and neck to saddle-leather brown. His eyes were a crackling blue, set wide over high cheekbones. Only the bright flame of his thick-cropped hair gave sure sign of his Celtic ancestry.

He took a small hip flask of whiskey from his saddlebag and poured it into the wash bowl sitting on the commode. Cutting it only slightly with water from the pitcher beside the bowl, he used his bandanna to give himself a brisk and thorough whore's bath. The raw whiskey made his skin tingle and, when he had finished, he was sure he could make it through to the next day when he would have the time to soak himself in a barber's hot tub.

Towelling himself dry, he tugged on his britches and put on a clean shirt, knotting a dark string tie at his throat. After stamping on his boots, he buckled on his gunbelt and holster, a new rig he had purchased in Santa Fe, dropped his big ivory-handled Colt into the holster, clapped on his hat, and left the room to get something to eat.

By this time, he was about ready to devour a full steer.

Downstairs in the hotel's dining room, he found a table, gave his order to the waitress, then slumped back in his seat, fully enjoying the luxury that followed a long ride. Crossing that blistering plateau had made him feel like a board that had laid out in the sun too long—brittle and maybe just a mite warped. His steak and fries and thick slabs of bread arrived, and he ate with gusto, after which he leaned back and ordered more coffee.

The coffee finished, he was about to leave for his appointment with Seth Barton when he saw a strikingly handsome woman pause in the dining room doorway. Her Irish heritage was obvious and something in the way she let her proud, dark eyes sweep the room—her cool imperiousness—would not let Canyon look away, the strength in her drawing him like a magnet. Though every bit a mature woman, she was still young, with thick, dark brown hair and a lush, full ripeness to her upper body. At the moment her lips, full and passionate, were set with iron resolve, her manner coolly indifferent to the gaze of the many male diners looking boldly at her from their tables.

She left the doorway and moved toward Canyon, taking a table close by his, a woman eating alone, but doing so without pause or reflection. As she made herself comfortable, Canyon kept his eyes boldly on her. Catching his glance, she did not look away, her gaze as direct as his own. Her eyes were luminous now with a bold challenge. She obviously knew she was beautiful and framed her picture for his glance—and that of every other man in the dining room. Her assurance was almost arrogant, and Canyon knew that few men had ever been able to match the bold, open challenge she presented—a challenge that now aroused more than his interest. He wished that the nature of his business in this town did not make it impossible for him to know this woman.

He dropped enough silver coins on the table to cover his meal, then left the dining room and mounted the stairs to the third floor. He proceeded to the end of a dim hallway, found room 25, and knocked. There was no answer. He knocked again, then tried the door. It was locked. He was too early, then. He proceeded to his own room and dropped onto the bed, crossing his arms behind his back while he gave Barton a chance to get to his room. After a good fifteen minutes, he left his room and knocked a second time on room 25. When he got no response this time, he became irritated—then somewhat apprehensive.

Back in his room, he heard a sudden uproar from the saloon across the street. He went to the window and looked down. Two men spilled out of the saloon and into the street, brawling wildly. Recognizing Seth Barton as one of the two men, Canyon cursed aloud. The president's agent was in a battle he had no chance of winning. His opponent was an oversized bull of a man dressed in a logger's wool hat and jacket. Swarming out of the saloon after them came a noisy crowd, its members urging on the two combatants with wild, shrill cries. In the street now, the two men fought toe to toe, grunting explosively with each crunching blow. Shouts of surprise and even approval sprang from the encircling crowd as the lighter Barton got in his licks. Even so, it was clear to every one in the crowd that the big logger would have no problem disposing of his opponent, and they were delighted to cheer the two men on. Nothing, Canyon knew, so warmed the heart of a saloon's population than the sight of blood—someone else's blood.

What had happened was obvious.

This fight was no accident, coming as it did so close after Canyon's arrival. Seth Barton's secret mission was secret no longer. He must have been spotted from the first as he nosed about seeking information on Caulder's whereabouts. With Canyon's arrival, the time had come for Caulder's forces to move in on Barton and his confederate. And this shaggy buffalo of a man pummeling Seth Barton in the street below was just the opening round.

Canyon left his room, plunged down the stairs out of the hotel and bulled his way through the crowd. Barton was down by this time, twisting slowly, painfully, while his opponent amused himself by kicking him repeatedly in the ribs with his steel-toed boots. Canyon grabbed the logger by the arm and swung him around. The logger flung up his forearms and managed to ward off Canyon's first punch. Canyon felt his clenched fist slam into the fellow's meaty, tree-branch of an arm—the recoil traveling clear back to his shoulder. Grinning, the giant shook off the blow and advanced on Canyon, who promptly took a few quick steps back to give himself room.

As he did so, he felt under his feet the sudden pound of hoofbeats. Glancing away from the logger, he saw the crowd melting hastily away before a solid phalanx of horsemen keeping solidly abreast as they charged down the street. The logger swung once at Canyon, then turned and bolted for the sidewalk as the hard-charging riders bore down on Canyon and the downed Seth Barton.

One of the men in the first rank was the dust-covered rider who had followed Canyon from Santa Fe. Rushing to Barton's side, Canyon grabbed him under the armpits and tried to drag him out of the path of the oncoming riders. But he saw he did not have enough time. The tide of horsemen was almost on them. He drew his Colt and fired up at the closest rider. The round went high and, before he could get off another shot, the storm of horsemen was on them. He flung himself upright and made a dash for the sidewalk. A horse loomed before him, its chest slamming his shoulder, the force of it enough to send him spinning violently up onto the wooden sidewalk, close by the mouth of an alley. He got up, stumbled, lost his balance, and plunged headlong.

His head struck the hard, unyielding corner of a building. His senses reeling from the blow, he pulled himself up in time to see the riders, wheeling back around now, coming after him. He managed to lift his Colt, but it seemed to weigh a ton. The scent of a woman fell over him and he felt strong hands grab him from behind and yank him farther into the alley. A second later he was pulled up onto a back porch, a door was opened, and he went stumbling into a small kitchen. He was helped into a kitchen chair. Turning about, he saw that he had been saved by the same woman he had noticed in the hotel dining room.

As he watched, still shaky, she slammed shut the kitchen door.

"No more heroics, mister," she told him. "Keep your head down and your mouth shut and let me handle this."

She snatched up a Greener that had been leaning in a corner and turned to face the door as heavy boots tramped up onto the small porch. There was a momentary pause. Canyon heard clearly the grating of harsh voices as the men crowding the porch debated what to do next. Then came the pound of fists on the door.

"You got him in there, Belle?"

"What if I have, Karl?"

"Damn you! You got no right sticking your nose into this."

"Get off my porch or I'll blow a hole in you!"

The angry fists began pounding on the door again.

"This Greener's loaded!" Belle warned.

"This ain't none of your business!"

"I'm making it my business. This here Greener's

loaded with double-ought buckshot. It'll tear a hole in this door and your belly besides. They'll have to pick you off that wall behind you."

"You're bluffin', Belle!"

She stepped to the window and blew it out with one barrel. Shards of glass and pieces of shattered window sash exploded into the alley. Before the echo of the awesome detonation died, she stepped back in front of the door.

"I ain't goin' to tell you again, Karl!" she cried, her voice resonant with resolve.

That announcement was unnecessary. Heavy boots were already pounding down the porch steps, and a moment later, Canyon heard the man she had called Karl shouting to his riders to saddle up, followed by the clatter of departing horses. As the riders galloped rode out of town, someone sent a round into the night sky out of pure frustration. Then came silence—a hushed, waiting silence broken only by a few distant shouts.

Canyon slumped back in the chair, his head buzzing, and thought of Seth Barton's trampled figure lying out there in the street. Then a great weariness turned his limbs to stone and he let his head sink down onto the table, aware for the first time of a gash in the side of his head, its warm blood trickling down his neck. Only dimly was he aware of the woman yanking him upright, then steering his tall, stumbling frame through a bedroom doorway. The last thing he recalled was flopping loosely back onto a bed while the woman wrapped a towel around his head, then cursed off his boots and tight britches.

2

The sun spilling into the bedroom momentarily blinded Canyon. He shook his aching head and squinted up at Belle. The tray she was carrying contained coffee, a platter of fried eggs and bacon, and thick slabs of toast spread with honey. The mug of coffee was steaming. He reached up and took it off the tray as she set it down on the night stand beside his bed.

"This coffee'll do for now," Canyon told her. "Soon's I get dressed, I'll finish off that platter out in the kitchen," he told her, cradling the hot coffee in both hands. "Never could manage eating in bed." Aware suddenly of the bandage wrapped about his head, he asked, "How long've I been here?"

"Two days."

"Must have been a nuisance. Sorry."

"No apologies needed."

"What about Seth Barton?"

"The man who was brawling with Bull Renfrew?"

"If that's the logger's name."

"That was Bull, all right. Your friend is torn up pretty bad. Those riders who ran him down did a good job. They broke two of his ribs and crushed a hip. He'll live, but he won't be sitting a horse so good after this."

"Jesus. Who's taking care of Barton?"

"Doc Sanderson. He's got an office over the barber shop and some spare beds in a back room. Barton should be safe enough there."

Canyon nodded. What little he had seen of Seth Barton he had liked. But the man had been careless. It had cost him—and almost cost Canyon, too.

"I thought I heard hammering just now," Canyon said, "coming from the kitchen."

"The carpenter's putting in a new window."

"Oh, yes," Canyon said, his blue eyes dancing as he appraised her admiringly. "I remember now. You blasted it with your Greener."

"It was just a bluff."

"A good one, as I recall. It did the trick."

"So far, yes."

"Belle, how come you've thrown in with me like this?"

She shrugged and picked up his tray. "Let's just say I don't like the way so many of these ex-Confederates have moved in here and taken over." She started for the door. "Your clothes are over there on the chair. And that big ivory-handled revolver."

"Thanks. It comes in handy sometimes."

"I can imagine." She paused with one hand on the doorknob. "You're breakfast will be waiting for you in the dining room. The carpenter is still working in the kitchen."

"All right, Belle. Thank you."

She left, pulling the door shut behind her.

* * *

Belle had placed another plate over the platter to keep the bacon and eggs warm. But it would not have mattered if she hadn't done so, Canyon was that famished. He breakfasted with gusto, then leaned back in his chair, feeling considerably better, though his head still ached slightly.

The woman's full name was Belle Summerfield, and it turned out she owned not only the Owl Hoot saloon, but the hotel, the feed mill, and a general store—all of them acquired over time in payment for gambling debts.

"You knew I was here to see Barton," he suggested to Belle, "the moment you spotted me in the restaurant. Right?"

She shrugged. "Seth is a nice enough fellow," she replied. "But he's not very good at keeping secrets. It wasn't long before everyone knew he was looking for Lance Caulder."

"I see."

"And God knows how many of Caulder's men saw him pause on the saloon's porch to speak to you." She smiled wryly at Seth's lack of good sense. "Lance knew he was waiting for someone, so when you showed up, he made his move. After all, you were only the second stranger in town in three weeks."

"With Seth being the first."

"Yes."

"Well, he'll have plenty of time to think on that now. Who was that rider who tracked me from Santa Fe?"

"Slim Winner. Lance sent him there to see who Seth was waiting for. When Slim rode into town on your heels, the party was on. For almost a week now, Lance Caulder's men had been drifting into town waiting for this."

"And now I've put you square in the middle of all this unpleasantness. I am sorry, Belle."

"No need to be. That's where I've always been. That's where this town sits, between the hill ranchers who came first and the big cattlemen beyond the range, who came here four years ago to fatten beef for the Confederacy—and making no bones about where they stand. To hear them tell it, they haven't yet lost the war."

"What's your stake in all this?"

"As I told you, I own a good chunk of this town—and it serves everyone's best interest to let me and the town alone so it can function properly, providing supplies and goods for the ranchers." She paused, her dark brows knitting. "And there's one more thing. Lance Caulder's asked me to marry him."

Canyon's eyebrows shot up. "And would you be giving that serious thought?"

She smiled, a cold light gleaming in her eyes. "Lance's finally swallowed his pride enough to make an offer to a woman who owns the best saloon and cathouse in town. It took a while for him to come around, but he's done so."

"And you want that?"

"He's a man needs to be taken down a peg," she said coldly. "And I'm just the woman to do it. That's what I want."

"To bring him down a peg."

"Yes."

"Sticking your neck out for me could mess things up."

"Let it, then. If he's that much of a fool, I don't want him."

"You sure you do want him, anyway, Belle? It doesn't sound to me that you care all that much about him. You're just interested in his come-uppance."

She sighed. "The man would be impossible, otherwise. He needs to be cut down to size. And besides, there comes a time when a woman's got to make the best deal she can. I ain't gettin' any younger. I'll be gettin' pretty worn around the edges before long."

"Looks to me like that's a long way off, Belle. At least, from where I'm sitting."

She smiled, boldly, appreciatively. "Nice of you to say that."

"I meant every word."

"I know you did, Canyon. And I appreciate it. Now you listen to me. I think you should make tracks from Placer Town—and fast. I know Lance. He has no intention of letting you out of here alive."

"Lance Caulder rode with Quantrill. And when he rode out on his own, he murdered and pillaged, killing innocent men, women, and children—and in one notorious case, over fifty captured Union prisoners. I'm not leaving here without him."

Belle frowned. "Talk hereabouts is that Lance had nothing to do with those atrocities—that it was all Quantrill's work."

"I know differently."

"But it was the war. In war, men do terrible things."

"Yes. Terrible things."

28

She leaned back in her chair. "I think I should warn you. You won't get any help from the local law. The town marshal and the sheriff are both in Lance's back pocket. Bought and paid for."

"I know that."

"You're crazy then if you think one man can bring him in. Maybe I shouldn't have helped you," she said ruefully. "All I've done is delay the inevitable. Lance will kill you."

"Don't bet on it, Belle. I might surprise you."

She frowned, obviously troubled at his obstinacy—but he thought he saw a flicker of admiration in her dark eyes, along with a touch of Ireland, as well.

Canyon got to his feet. "There's just one thing I really need," he said, smiling down at her, "before I move on out of here."

She stood up also. "And what might that be?"

"A good hot bath. I've been needing one since I rode in."

"There's a tub in the back room. I'll send over one of my girls to fill it. She'll even scrub your back, if you want."

He smiled into her flashing eyes. "Now that's a chore I was hoping you'd be taking care of," he told her impishly.

"Well now, you crazy Irishman," she said, brightening. "That might be arranged."

He stepped toward her. She did not retreat. Her lips were slightly apart, glistening with moisture. It would take but a nudge to open them. She had to lift her head to meet his gaze, and suddenly her eyes were heavy and the veiled expression broke. He saw naked, eager want—deep and powerful—

flood into them. He put his hands on her hips and nudged her closer until her full thighs pressed against his. Then he kissed her full on the lips—and found them opening with a warmth and urgency that stirred his groin to life.

Her eyes grew darker as she pushed him gently away. The self-confidence in them grew oddly bitter. "You did that easily enough," she said, her voice soft with anger. "I warn you, Canyon. I am not easy. Not to any man."

"I didn't think you were," he told her, smiling amiably at her, refusing to take offense. "Back at that restaurant I was sorry I wouldn't be seeing you again. Despite everything, I'm glad it didn't work out that way."

She took a step closer. "Then kiss me again," she told him, the anger in her voice gone now. "Then I'll get the water for your bath. And maybe I'll take one with you."

"I'd like that."

"Kiss me, damn you," she said. "And shut up."

He took her in his arms and did as she bid.

They were both still damp from their bath when they struck the silken coverlet of Belle's canopied bed. They had been teasing each other during the bath, and now, coming to rest on the bed, they were feverish with their need for each other.

Her arms around his neck, Belle drew him hungrily down onto her lips. He kissed her with a hungry savagery, his lips pressing her mouth open wider. He sent his tongue darting in boldly and felt her pull back momentarily, as if the shock of his raw urgency had shaken her. But the hesitation gave way at once to a desire as fierce and demanding as his own, and she answered his thrusting tongue eagerly, wantonly.

Pulling back from the kiss, he grinned down at her and gazed appreciatively upon her lush ripeness. But she would have no pause now and pulled him down onto her breasts with a fierceness that amused him. She thrust one of her breasts into his mouth. He took the nipple and let his tongue encircle the flat tip, then flick it repeatedly until it came fully to attention, allowing him to enclose it gently but firmly between his teasing teeth. She gasped, her arms tightening convulsively about him.

Chuckling, he pushed himself atop her and let his throbbing shaft nudge against her moist, silken muff. Eagerly, she opened her thighs to him. He plunged in, driving hard and deep. A delighted gasp broke from her. Her nails raked his back. Still thrusting deeply, he leaned back enough to grab one of her breasts in his big hand and squeeze. A radiant glow suffused her face.

"No more play!" she told him, almost angrily. "Give it to me!"

Obedient to her cry—and to his own needs, he did as she pleaded, and in a moment was no longer thinking of her, but only of his own urgency as he pounded into her. She bucked under him, her head thrashing from side to side, intent on crossing that barrier—until at last she cried out unashamedly and they plunged over the top together and became lost in the searing urgency of their mutual spasms.

When it was done for him, he let himself sag forward onto her warm lushness, panting slightly, aware of the rosy glow that had suffused her face and of the fine beads of moisture that covered her milk-white shoulders and breasts.

"You had enough, Belle?"

"Don't ask foolish questions. Someday I'll meet a man who won't roll over and start snoring on me."

"Maybe you already have."

"Show me."

Chuckling, he leaned back and gazed upon her. She let him, making no effort at all to pull a sheet over her. "Just let me look first," he told her. "That helps, you know."

She looked back at him just as boldly. "I don't mind. A woman likes to feel a man's eyes on her nakedness. It's something we need as much as you do."

It was still difficult for him to believe the full, wondrous ripeness of her, the silken, ample breasts, her narrow waist and flaring hips, in the valley of which rested the lush, dark mystery of her gleaming nap. It was no wonder that when she entered that dining room not a single man in it could look away.

"Finished?" she asked.

"You mean am I ready again?"

"You know what I mean."

She seemed to be panting, like a great she-cougar after a long run. He rested his hand on her moist patch, then let his fingers nudge past the lips and slip inside.

She moaned, her red tongue flicking over her lips. "Hurry up, damn you, Canyon," she whispered huskily, her voice heavy with urgency. "I can't wait any longer!"

He swung onto her once more, his thrusting erection sinking deep into her moist warmth. With an exultant cry, she sucked him in still deeper. Amazed at her swift readiness, he hung back and looked down at her, a teasing smile on his face.

"You sure you're ready for this?"

"Yes, damn you!" she hissed. "Yes!"

He drove hard into her, drew back, and drove in again, each thrust punctuated by her deep, guttural gasps of pleasure. Every part of her body responded, her hot flesh beyond control now, her nails raking up and down his back in a kind of fierce, mindless passion. In the mounting frenzy of her coming, she tossed her head wildly back and forth, her bright, white teeth clenched.

Soon, he too was caught up in her wildness. They flung themselves at each other in a mindless, thrusting dance that knew no deliberation—only raw need. Her muted cries grew stronger, then they shattered the room's heaving silence. Her fingers digging into his legs, her body plunging upward, she cried out with a piercing shriek that seemed to be wrung from the deepest coils of her being, the cry trailing away into a long, soft moan. Canyon remained poised deep within her, the unbearable tension in his groin ripping at him as he lunged still deeper for one more final, explosive thrust—and then he exploded, expending his seed within her throbbing warmth in a series of pulsing thrusts that caused him to cry out with the sheer relief of it.

She would not let him go, keeping him deep

within her as her womb drank in all that he had to offer. Leaning back, he gazed deeply into her smoky dark eyes and smiled.

"You all right, Belle?" he inquired.

"Oh, God," she moaned softly as she shuddered involuntarily, her abdomen sucking in, then out— her body caught up in a delayed orgasm.

He pressed his cheek down on her warm breasts and waited. At last, with a deep sigh, her hand came down to caress his back and shoulder. It was then she felt the long ridges her nails had left.

"My poor dear, have I torn up your back?"

"I'll live."

As he pulled gently back, she turned in his arms and pulled his face close to hers, kissing him hungrily, her lips soft and pliant.

"Thank you, Canyon. That was lovely."

"You see, I didn't roll over and go to sleep."

"No, you didn't, and that's a fact." She touched his head gingerly, caressing the spot where it had struck. "How's that nasty gash?"

"No bother."

"Good. I wouldn't want that to slow you down any."

"You mean you're not finished yet?"

She laughed softly. "Of course not."

"Do your damndest," he told her. "I'll hope for the best."

With a soft, deep laugh, she moved on top of him, prowling over him like a big cat, her molten lips enclosing his. Then, gently, she eased back until she found his growing erection and with swift fingers guided him into her. With an explosive sigh, she eased herself slowly back and sucked him in still deeper, smiling down at him from a great height, her dark, fragrant hair spilling about him like a tent. Astonishingly, he felt the hard barrel of his shaft growing as it thrust deeper and still deeper into her.

Pleased at his resurrection, she laughed again, a deep, husky laugh. "You see what happens when I do my damndest?"

"I'm still hoping," he told her.

She leaned her head back and began rocking slowly back and forth. "Don't worry, Canyon," she told him between clenched teeth.

He didn't. The intensity of her rocking increased gradually, and it soon became obvious that he was going to have no trouble—as the surging intensity of their lovemaking increased. Reaching up, he cupped her breasts in his own big hands, once more losing himself in the savage intensity of their coupling as he thrust himself brutally up into her, until at last the storm had passed.

This time Belle collapsed forward onto the bed beside him, entirely spent—like a long-distance runner just crossing the finish line. A drugged, heavy-lidded exhaustion claimed Canyon as well; and, firmly clasped in each other's arms, they drifted off into a deep, delicious sleep.

The last thing Canyon remembered was realizing how hungry he had become all over again.

3

With Belle in the kitchen preparing them both a much-needed second breakfast, Canyon sat at the dining room table, sipping coffee and considering his options. It was a consideration that led him to the obvious conclusion that his best bet from here on would be to ally himself with those hill ranchers who might stand with him against Lance Caulder and the rest of the Confederate sympathizers.

Belle had already told him that Caulder owned the largest spread of all, a ranch he called Dixieland, his brand—naturally enough—the Confederate bars. The Dixieland riders numbered almost twenty, Belle told him, and this body of men, added to those riders with the other cattlemen allied with him, amounted to a formidable force. Alone, Canyon was far too vulnerable; Seth Barton's condition was clear evidence of that.

Belle brought in their platter of steak, fries, and toast and joined him at the table. A few minutes into it, Canyon asked Belle to give him a picture of the situation between the hill ranchers and the other cattlemen. "You made it sound like two warring groups before," he reminded her.

"That's just what we have up here," she told

him, filling his cup with fresh coffee. "The hill ranchers are struggling to survive, running cattle on pasture that is considerably smaller and less productive than those on the other side of the range."

"That's the luck of the draw, isn't it? Why should that be the source of conflict?"

"The big cattlemen say they're losing stock to the hill ranchers."

"Are they?"

Belle shrugged. "Could be."

"In that case, why don't Caulder and the other cattlemen band together to stop them?"

"So far Caulder has kept out of it. He and the other cattlemen have more than enough stock, anyway. Except for Jim Swallows of the Box J. And he doesn't count."

"Why not?"

"He's not one of those ex-Confederates who came in here with Caulder."

"And the others are, so they dance to Caulder's tune."

"Yes."

For a while the two ate silently, but with real gusto, their recent acrobatics having aroused their appetites to a remarkable pitch. After swabbing his plate clean with a slice of bread, Canyon finished his coffee and leaned back to gaze thoughtfully at Belle. "What can you tell me about these hill ranchers? Do you know any of them?"

"I know all of them. There's more of them than the others, and I depend on them for most of my business."

"Who's their leader?"

"They don't really have one when it comes to that. They're all pretty independent. But in a pinch I'd say Sam Gills of the Lazy S would be the one most likely to come forward and take charge."

"Is he mixed up in this rustling, do you think?"

"He says he's not," she said. "But when I consider that crew of his, I'm pretty sure he's up to something. He has more men than he needs for the size of his spread. And there are times when his crew really thins out—like most of them are off somewhere."

"You mean off driving rustled cattle to a buyer."

"Yes."

"Where would they find a buyer out here?"

"There's a town in the mountains a good deal west of here—a mining town. What I hear is buyers are always on hand there to purchase any cattle a crew can drive there for sale to the mining camps in Utah and Arizona—even as far as California, no questions asked."

"What's the name of this place?"

"Silver Creek," She told him, filling her own cup with fresh coffee.

Canyon considered. What Sam Gills was really up to was not his concern, so long as the man had the manpower—and the will—to stand up to Lance Caulder. Canyon was here to bring in Caulder, and all other considerations were beside the point. His next move then had to be to get free of this town and seek out the Lazy S.

"Could you steer me to Sam Gills's ranch?" he asked Belle.

"From what I hear you just stay on the road

you took riding in here until you're pretty deep into the mountains. Gills is supposed to have built himself a big log house on the end of a long bench-land, high on a bluff. You can't miss it, I hear—once you get that far."

"Any other ranches I might pass?"

"The Steadman place. Sun Ranch."

"How long a ride is it to the Lazy S?"

"Once past the Steadman place, I'd say two more days at least. You'll find yourself in steep, rough country, Canyon. Sam likes his privacy, so you won't find him very sociable."

"I guess I can understand that."

"You won't heed my warning?"

"You mean go back without Lance Caulder?"

"Yes."

"Of course not."

"You're a stubborn man."

Canyon finished his coffee and got to his feet. "Before I set out, I've got to see how Seth's doing."

Belle got up also. "I'll go with you."

Doc Sanderson was not a very impressive-looking man of medicine. His sunken cheeks were rosy with the hectic flush of the consumptive. A nearly empty bottle of whiskey sat on his desk, a tin cup beside it. The office itself was a shambles.

Too disorganized to shake Canyon's hand when Belle introduced him, he mumbled something apologetic about the office's appearance and made a feeble effort to clear off his desk. Then, running long fingers through his thinning hair, he led Canyon and Belle into the room where Seth Barton was recuperating. Barton did not look good. His face was still swollen from the beating he had suffered at the hands of the logger, and his head and ribs were tightly bandaged. His back propped up by two large pillows, he was staring morosely out through a dirty window when Belle, followed by Canyon, entered the long attic room.

Canyon stopped by the cot. "How you feelin', Seth?"

"I've felt better. The doc here says my hip's broke."

"Along with a couple of ribs," Doc Sanderson said, stepping closer.

"What're you goin' to do now, Canyon?" Barton asked.

"I'm not exactly sure. But I'm riding out soon to look the country over—see what I can find. Allies, maybe."

"Sure wish I could go with you."

"Stay put. Soon's I get back, we'll put you on a train."

"That can wait. Just get Lance Caulder for me."

Canyon clapped Barton on the shoulder. "Rest easy, Seth. I'll be doing whatever I can. But nailing this man won't be all that easy, I'm thinking."

Canyon nodded to Belle, then followed her and the doctor from the room.

"He'll be all right," the doc said, walking with them to the outer door. "He's been hurt bad, but I figure he'll be able to ride in a couple of weeks, maybe a month."

"I should be back in plenty of time to give him a hand, doc. Meanwhile, take good care of him."

"If you need anything, doctor," said Belle, "get in touch with me."

"All right, Belle."

Canyon clapped on his hat, left the office, and moved down the outside wooden steps with Belle. At the bottom, Belle paused to squint through the late afternoon sunshine at Canyon.

"It's late. Do you really have to leave today?"

"I want to get on with this, Belle. I've already given Lance Caulder too much time to think. He knows I'm here."

"He might kill you."

Canyon shrugged. "I don't get killed easy. That's a promise, lass."

"Is it that important—that you bring Lance in. The war's over."

"For some, maybe. But not for those with long memories. And the U.S. government has such a memory."

"I find it hard to believe Lance was responsible for those atrocities. I think if you knew the man you'd think differently. He's tough. But he's not the kind of man you described to me."

"And yet he's a man you want to bring down a peg."

"Only to make him more tractable."

"You can't tame a mad dog, Belle. And if you don't believe he's what I say he is, go on back upstairs and visit with Seth Barton."

She started to respond, but he held up his hand and smiled, unwilling to continue the discussion. He said gently, "I'll be pushing off now, Belle. Thanks—for everything."

"You're as stubborn as a mule, Canyon. But stubborn or not, I'll be looking forward to seeing you again."

He grinned. "And I'll sure be looking forward to another hot bath."

She kicked him in the shins—gently.

Canyon didn't get far that day, as he knew he wouldn't; but he slept well enough under the stars, and at the first light of dawn set out, following the road all the way through the canyon, lifting out of it gradually until he came to a creek boiling violently down the mountain side. He crossed a gravel ford and, disregarding Belle's advice, left the road. Deep in the pines he built a small fire, cooked bacon and coffee and shaved, then resumed his journey.

The sun hung high above the pines, the western slope up which the palomino toiled still gray and cold. There was almost no underbrush. The red pines crowded thickly about him, the almost solid mat of their branches trapping the sun's rays. A thousand years of needle-fall made a spongy surface upon which the horse's feet struck with scarcely a sound. Except for the slight jingle of the bridle metal and the occasional distant tap of a woodpecker's bill, a primeval stillness hung over the timbered slope.

Every now and then he passed over narrow buffalo and game trails cut out of the side of the slopes. He followed them for a while when it took him in the direction he wanted to go and rode without haste to save the palomino, stopping frequently to let it blow. As he rode, he found himself thinking of Belle—and of her need to believe that Lance Caulder had been only one minor actor in the Confederate bushwhackers' tale of rapine and murder, that Quantrill and not Caulder was responsible for the mayhem. She was right about Quantrill, of course; but unfortunately Lance Caulder had proved himself to be an apt pupil of that hellish marauder.

At noon he dismounted before another creek, rested, and resumed his journey. After the first quick rise beyond the canyon, the mountain slopes began to break into benches where short-grass meadows and finger-shaped valleys lay between the green patches of timber. He crossed these openly, still high above the road, reached timber, and climbed again to the next higher bench. The road he had left suddenly swung into sight on the slopes below him. Thus far, the timber had furnished good traveling, but at this point the steep slopes began to break into canyons and sharp-backed ridges, through which the road made the only comfortable passage.

He returned to it therefore, and sunset found him camped beside a swift mountain stream just above it. He picketed his horse in a small flat and made his meal. Then he built up the fire larger than he needed, drew his blankets beyond the fire's glow and watched the world plunge into darkness. Swarms of stars flickered in the heavens above him, beckoning to him. He seemed to feel the earth turning under him, as a gentle wind, chilled at this elevation, brushed his cheek. What light there was came from a thin sliver of a moon tiltled low to the southwest.

He could make out the road's pale surface just below him. Close by, he knew, there had to be ranch quarters. Riders would pass and see his fire, perhaps—and this was his intention. He took out his pipe and smoked it, enjoying the ease that comes after a long day's ride. He finished the pipe, knocked out the spent tobacco, and turned in.

Not long after, he heard the run of a horse far down the road. He turned in his blanket, reached for his Henry, and threw a handful of pine needles on the fire. The blaze crackled and lifted its light against the darkness. He listened to the horse come on and lay flat on his back with his feet toward the fire, his head against the saddle, the rifle on the ground beside him, his finger resting on the trigger. The rider came quickly around a bend in the road, reached a point just below him and pulled to a halt at sight of the blazing campfire.

Canyon saw the rider's shape bend in the saddle and heard the squeak of saddle leather as a woman's voice came to him out of the darkness:

"Hello, up there!"

She sat still on the sidesaddle. In the dim moonlight, he could barely make out her tan shirt and long, dark riding skirt and a man's hat sitting back on her head. He said hello back at her and she guided her mount off the road and up the steep grade until she was close enough for him to see the graceful curve of her neck and the dark honey of her long hair as she craned to see him behind the leaping fire.

"You don't make sense, mister."

"What kind of sense you lookin' for, ma'am?"

"You keep away from the road all day, as if you were on the run. Then you camp here where everybody can see you and build a fire big as a house. And now you keep yourself back in the shadows so a body can't get a look at you."

She was nervous, he realized, and was really asking if maybe he had a gun trained on her. "Relax," he told her, sitting up. "And tell me how you know I left the road?"

"I saw you a while back and followed—from a safe distance, of course."

"Why?"

"I was curious."

"That's no answer, but let that go for now."

"You didn't think you could ride this far into these hills without anyone noticing, did you?"

"I'm not on the run, if that's what's bothering you."

Canyon got slowly to his feet. He saw her stiffen some as she took note of his tall figure. He smiled, his teeth a white gleam against the shadows of his face, the fire throwing into sharp relief its rugged planes. Her eyes narrowed in quick appraisal. She seemed pleased with what she saw.

"This is no place to camp," she told him. "You'd get a bullet in that fire before another hour had passed."

"What do you suggest?"

"It's too dangerous for a stranger out here. Saddle up and come to our ranch."

"And what ranch might that be?"

"Sun Ranch."

He saw her eyes narrow suddenly as she got a better look at him and realized there was something in his appearance which told her who he was. "Are you the one who tried to stop Bull from beating up that fellow the other night?"

Canyon nodded. "You know that big logger?"

"I know him. But he's no logger. Just a bully in Lance Caulder's employ."

"My friend didn't do too well."

"That's no wonder. My father was in town when it happened. He told me about it. No one has ever been able to stop Bull."

Suddenly, from the east, the rapid drumming of horse's hooves filled the night.

"Saddle up and kick out the fire," the girl said impatiently.

He made up his blanket roll in quick turns, threw on the saddle and lashed his roll. He gave the fire a quick, sideways kick with his boot, sending the blazing firewood into the stream. Then, mounting up, he let her take the lead as she moved ahead of him up the slope. At the top of the grade they crossed a narrow flat and kept on into the timber. She halted then and they sat their horses, listening. A moment later a storm of horsemen swept past them along the road far below them and disappeared into the night.

"They'll be at the ranch waiting for us," she told him.

"Friends?"

"No. Lance Caulder's men."

"Then let's go," he said.

They descended to the road and kept on it through a shallow canyon, still rising into the cool night. Reaching a level area surrounded by the shadow of ragged hills, they crossed a creek making a swift, smooth run across their paths. Lights gleamed ahead and Canyon saw shapes cut in front of them, moving across a yard—the riders that had plunged out of the night behind them earlier. A plank bridge boomed a warning of their approach, and soon they were approaching a log house built low and long across the yard. Four sweaty horses were standing at the hitch rack, their tails drooping wearily.

The huge square shape of a man stood in the lighted doorway, peering out at them. They pulled to a halt in front of the low porch and dismounted. The big man moved out onto the porch. Stepping through the doorway after him came another man, tall, slim, his square face clean-shaven, his eyes cold. He wore his arrogance like a badge.

Canyon was finally about to meet Lance Caulder.

As Canyon and the woman approached the porch steps, two other men crowded out onto the porch with Caulder. One of them was the big logger, Bull Renfrew. The other one was a stranger to Canyon.

The woman who had brought Canyon in said, "I came on this man above the road, Dad. He needs a place to sleep and a meal."

The big, blocky man brushed past Lance Caulder to the edge of the porch to peer closely down at Canyon. "My name's Steadman, mister. And that's my daughter Helen just brought you in. What's your name?"

"Canyon O'Grady."

"You in these hills to cause trouble, are you?"

Canyon glanced over at Lance Caulder, then looked back at Steadman. "If I don't get any trouble from you or these men with you," he said laconically, "I don't see why I should cause any."

"Fair enough," pronounced Steadman. He glanced

at his daughter. "Show O'Grady to the bunkhouse, Helen. You done right. Strangers are welcome. Take him to the cookhouse when he's settled and see he gets a hot cup o' coffee."

"Hold it right there, Steadman," Lance Caulder snapped. "Ah know what this stranger's doin' here. He's a damn Yankee just rode in to bring me trouble."

Steadman swung around to look at Canyon, a bit more closely this time. "That right, mister?"

"Right enough. Lance Caulder was a Confederate bushwhacker. He outdid Quantrill and he's got some answering to do for that."

"The war's over, mister—or ain't you heard."

"I heard."

"Well, then, it won't do much good for you to chew on that cud any more. I say you're still welcome to the bunk and the coffee, but I suggest you move on first thing in the morning. Be better for all concerned."

"Come on, Mr. O'Grady," Helen said to Canyon.

She walked with him to the barn and waited outside while Canyon stabled the palomino, then accompanied him across the yard to the bunkhouse.

"Dad's a good man, Mr. O'Grady," Helen said, her soft voice low. "But he's not about to take on Lance Caulder—not now, he isn't. All he wants is to live in peace and do what's right—so things will go well for me."

"It's not your father I'm after, Helen."

"But you can't go against Lance Caulder. He's much too powerful to tangle with. There's talk he'll be the territorial governor before long."

"I sincerely doubt that, Helen. But powerful or not, I'm going to have to do what is neccesary."

"Then watch out. You are in Lance Caulder's land now. You saw them when we rode up. Lance Caulder and his men were off their horses and into our house looking for you without a by-your-leave. Afterward, they barged out onto our porch like it was their own. Dad hates them, but there's nothing he can do to stop them. They take what they want without apology and ride out, immune from any prosecution. Even up here in these dark hills, the owner of the Dixieland ranch is king."

Frowning, Canyon glanced back at the ranch house. "Then I guess it took some guts for your father to offer his hospitality to me just now—and yours to bring me here in the first place. Once you got a good look at me, you knew who I was—and who you and your father would be going against. Is that right?"

They had reached the bunkhouse by this time. Helen paused in front of it. "Yes," she said, gazing calmly up at him. "I knew."

"I recognized Bull. Who were the others with Caulder?"

"The heavy-set one is Karl Berdick, the Dixieland foreman."

"Oh, yes. He was the one came after me when Belle Summerfield took me in hand. He has hard fists."

"Belle Summerfield . . . ?"

"Never mind. It's a long story."

She opened the bunkhouse door for him and stepped back. "If Juan's awake," she told him, "have him take you over to the cookshack. Good night, Mr. O'Grady."

"Good night, Helen."

Juan was a bent, white-haired old Mexican who had obviously ridden too many broncs in his time. After Canyon found himself a bunk, Juan put his teeth back in and escorted Canyon over to the cookshack. He left Canyon in the care of a tall cook, whose cadaverous appearance made Canyon wonder some about the quality of the food he provided for this crew.

The coffee was excellent, however, and Canyon was leaning against the cookshack doorway sipping it when Lance Caulder, flanked by Bull and the man Helen had identified as the foreman Karl Berdick, walked over to deal with him. Canyon was not surprised. He had been expecting this visit.

Caulder pulled to a halt in front of Canyon. "You all got a habit of hiding behind a woman's skirts, O'Grady," he told him, his southern drawl as thick as pudding. "But pretty soon your luck is going to run out."

Canyon sipped his coffee and smiled at Caulder, aware that the man had heard about his visit with Belle Summerfield—and did not like it one bit.

"Get a good rest tonight, O'Grady," Caulder continued, "because you'll be starting a long ride in the morning—all the way back to Placer City—and then Santa Fe."

"I'm not going back to Placer City or Santa Fe, and when I do, Caulder, it won't be alone."

"Brave words, O'Grady."

Canyon just shrugged.

"Then you insist on continuing on into these hills?"

"As long as this is still a free country."

Caulder's eyes narrowed. "You sayin' you got business up here with some of these pore white trash ranchers?"

Canyon just smiled at the man. Where he was heading—to Sam Gills ranch—and why, he had no intention of telling Caulder, or anyone else, for that matter.

Bull Renfrew stepped closer to Canyon. "Maybe you won't be goin' nowhere, you Yankee bastard."

"Ah'll handle this, Bull," said Caulder as he pulled the big logger back.

"I don't see why we're wastin' our time talkin' to this son of a bitch," broke in Karl Berdick, the foreman's beefy face flushing angrily. "Bull's right. We can put this Yankee vermin away right now, Lance."

"Shut up, Karl. Ah'll handle this."

"Then handle it," his foreman blurted angrily. "This son of a bitch is trouble!"

Lance swung around and slapped his foreman so hard the man's eyes teared from the blow. It looked for a second that he might spring on Caulder in retaliation, but he swallowed his anger and stepped almost meekly back.

"Ah won't tell you this again, Karl," Caulder told him coldly. "The man ain't born of woman can tell me what to do. So don't you try." He turned then to direct his gaze on Canyon.

"Ah know what you're up to, mister," he told Canyon, "and who sent you. Ah have powerful friends; so ah don't really have to worry all that much about you or that Tennessee turncoat says he's the president. The thing is, you all don't have any legal right to take me anywhere; and that's the pure and simple truth of it. So take mah advice. Stay away from Belle Summerfield and go back where you came from. These hills have hidden many a secret in years past. They can handle a few more."

He turned quickly about then and with Bull and his foreman headed back to their waiting horses. A moment later Canyon watched them gallop off into the night.

They had ridden into Placer Town to finish him off, Canyon realized, but had missed him there. When they finally overtook him in the hills, he was safe up up here in Steadman's place. If just now Lance Caulder had not dealt with him as Bull Renfrew wanted, it was only because he realized that Steadman and his daughter would be witnesses—and they were not the kind of people who could be bought off.

So Lance Caulder would have to wait for the proper moment—when the only witnesses would be those who gunned Canyon down.

4

Canyon ate breakfast in the cookshack with Stead-man's crew, then saddled his palomino and rode out of the barn into the bright morning's light, sucking in the mountain's thin, bracing air. In front of the corral, Steadman was meeting with his crew, giving them the day's assignments. The crew mounted up and moved off downgrade into the trees, not one of them glancing back at Canyon.

Helen appeared on the cabin's front porch, caught sight of Canyon and descended the steps, heading toward him. She was wearing her long riding skirt and carrying a riding crop. When she reached him, she asked impishly if he had appreciated spending the night under a roof.

"A welcome change, that I'll be admitting," Canyon told her, a twinkle in his blue eyes. "But the stars do make an uncommonly pretty roof."

She laughed. "Ride with me a ways," she said, moving past him to the barn.

In a moment, she led her saddled horse from the barn and mounted up. Canyon pulled alongside of her and they set off across a steep meadow, heading east. A narrow trace split the meadow. When they reached it, they followed it until it led into a heavy stand of timber. Slipping into its cool morning twilight, they kept going steadily upgrade.

"Where's this trace lead?" he asked.

"East over this range."

"Wrong direction, Helen. I'm staying on the road, heading northwest, for the Lazy S."

"That's not such a good idea."

"Why?"

"This morning Dad told me he overheard Lance Caulder making plans last night. He's gone after his crew. They should be waiting for you on the other road. The way they're planning it, you'll just disappear somewhere in these hills."

Canyon looked uneasily about him. There was no reason not to believe Helen. It sounded like just what Lance Caulder would do. Hell, from Caulder's standpoint, it made damn good sense.

"So what's your plan, Helen?"

"On the other side of this range, there's a cattle-man, Jim Swallows. Tell him I sent you."

"You trust him, do you?"

"He wants to marry me."

"And you'd be agreeing to the idea, would you now?"

"Yes, if it weren't for Dad. But Dad wouldn't hear of it."

"And why not?"

"Pride more than anything else. When Dad first came to these hills, he was hard scrabble, nothing on his back and a past not worth mentioning. So he built a cabin out of logs he cut with a hand ax and rustled cattle to give himself a start."

"And the cattle he . . . appropriated, they belonged to this here Jim Swallows."

"Yes. Though Dad only took enough to give himself a start, he still feels bad about it. It don't matter that Jim has long since forgiven Dad the few cattle he took. He can't look Jim in the face. He's got this stubborn pride."

"Helen, I wouldn't give a pinch of coon snuff for a man without pride—but sometimes it does make things a mite difficult."

"It surely does," she agreed somberly.

Reaching the crest of the trace up which their horses had been laboring, she halted and pointed to a tall pine atop a distant ridge. Blackened by a lightning bolt, it stood out starkly against the sky. "When you reach that pine, look northeast and you'll see a long flat. Keep on across the flat through a narrow pass. It's the only way out of this range without using the road. On the other side of the pass, you'll come to Jim Swallows's Box J outfit."

"You mean I'm to make a run for Swallows's ranch."

"It's not much help, I know; but it's all I can offer."

"I don't like the idea—running from Lance Caulder and his crew."

"There's that fool male pride again."

Canyon chuckled. "I suppose so."

"Jim will help you, I'm sure. He dislikes Lance Caulder almost as much as my father does. So why not give Jim a chance to help you? He'd appreciate it."

"All right, then. I'll do it. But there's just one thing I want you to do for me."

"Of course. What's that?"

"When Caulder rides back along the road looking for me, there's no doubt he's going to ask you which direction I took."

"I won't tell him."

"Yes, you will. Tell him. I'll have enough distance on him by that time, so it won't matter. If you try to deny you know which way I went, it could arouse Caulder to a fury and there's no telling what he might do. I've seen the records on that man. Believe me when I say he's dangerous."

Helen shuddered. "I believe you."

"I don't want you and your father to get into any more trouble with Caulder over me. Tell Caulder what he wants to know. Let him come after me, if he wants."

"All right. If you think that's best."

He smiled. "Thanks, Helen. And thank your father for me, too."

"I will, and say hello to Jim for me."

"I'll be sure to do that," he told her.

Touching his hat brim in salute to her, Canyon clapped heels to the palomino and continued on a hard run across the ridge to the pine Helen had indicated. When he reached it, he pulled up and looked back the way he had come. Helen was no longer in sight, and he saw no sign of pursuit.

That would come later.

He pulled his horse back around and set it on down the steep, heavily timbered slope until he reached the flat. Pulling up, he studied the distant pass. A ride straight across the flat to it would leave him in plain sight for too long a time—while if he remained in the timber, though it would take longer, it offered him concealment.

He wheeled the palomino and cut back into the

timber, keeping in it for close to three miles, then cut higher into the pines, urging the palomino on up the steep carpet of pine needles until he came to a sandstone ledge that loomed out of the mountainside like a huge, bleached collar bone. He dismounted and tethered the horse to a sapling, snaked the Henry from its scabbard, then moved up onto the shelf until he gained a clear view of the flat and the pass beyond. He crouched low and waited.

He didn't have long to wait.

Far to the west, as if they were flying from all the demons in hell, Caulder and his crew poured down through the timbered slopes and out onto the flat, a few of his men wearing what appeared to be remnants of their Confederate uniforms—caps and jackets mostly. Surging out across the flat, they headed directly for the pass. Canyon watched them sweep across the flat for a moment, then returned to his horse and, urging it still higher on the slope, found a brush-covered ridge line and held to it, his eye on the horsemen racing ahead of him across the flat.

When a sheer wall of rock blocked his way, he left the ridge and, still keeping in the timber, moved down through the timber to the flat and found that Caulder's crew had already vanished through the pass. He rode out onto the flat and kept on through the pass and came out onto a long, gently sloping plain. Far ahead of him, Caulder and his crew—now but a distant clot of riders—were heading northeast.

He cut across the broad, sweeping grassland, noting as he did the lush grass as high as the palomino's belly. No wonder the hill ranchers coveted the beef fattened on the succulent pastures of this plateau. He had not ridden far when he heard distant shouts. He glanced to the north. A sharp-eyed rider had caught sight of him, and his shouts were bringing the rest of Caulder's men back in Canyon's direction. He saw the riders snaking around in a long circle to cut him off.

Canyon bent low over his mount as he gave it its head, and before long caught sight of what he assumed was Jim Swallows's ranch buildings on a timbered ridge ahead of him. He kept on and was galloping into a long, low swale when from around a grassy knoll just ahead of him, four riders came charging directly at him. Canyon pulled to a halt as the lead rider circled him cautiously, his gun drawn. Though Canyon could not be certain, he assumed this was the owner of the Box J, Jim Swallows. Behind Swallows, his three companions reined in also, their eyes hard, questioning, as they peered at him. Still more riders came on them, materializing out of the tall grass with barely a sound.

"Who are you, mister?" the lead rider inquired.

"Name's O'Grady. I'm looking for the owner of the Box J. Would you be him?"

"I would," the man replied. "Name's Jim Swallows."

He thrust out a strong hand. Canyon shook it. The owner of the Box J rode tall in the saddle, a bony, loose-jointed fellow with a lantern jaw and a powerful hook of a nose. His eyes were dark and smoky—an Indian's eyes. Canyon liked the man at once.

"Helen Steadman sends her best wishes," he told Swallows.

"She sent you?"

Canyon nodded. "There's some unfriendlies on my tail, so she gave me directions to your place."

"We've already caught sight of them. Who are they?"

"Lance Caulder and his crew."

One of Swallows's riders had pulled up on a slight rise beyond them and was looking north. He called out to warn them that the riders were coming fast and hard. Swallows smiled, his teeth a white slash in his tanned face.

"Good," he said. He looked about at his men. "See to your weapons and stand fast."

As his men checked the loads in their revolvers, Swallows asked Canyon, "Why are they after you, O'Grady—if you don't mind my asking."

"I'm after bringing in Lance Caulder."

"Lance Caulder? Bring him in? Why?"

"For a trial, then a rope—if there's any justice, that is."

"Well, now. You don't fool around, do you. Bringing in Lance Caulder is a tall order in these parts."

"Sure, and that self-same thought has occurred to me, as well."

"Is this some private score you have to settle with that rattlesnake?"

"I regret I'm not at liberty to say much more than what I have just told you. Ask Lance Caulder, if you want. He seems to know who I am and who it was sent me."

"You a lawman?"

Canyon smiled. "I wish I could be of more help."

"Never mind. You've told me as much as I need to know. Any enemy of Lance Caulder is welcome at the Box J."

Swallows looked around at his men, their drawn six-guns gleaming in the sunlight. Each man seemed almost as eager to tangle with the Dixieland riders as did Swallows. Their mounts, which had caught the scent of the approaching horses, were already getting skittish.

"Dismount and spread out," Swallows told his men. "Keep low in the grass. Like a fishnet in the sea." He glanced over at Canyon. "Stick by me, O'Grady, in case hot lead starts flying."

"I hope it won't come to that."

Swallows's men dismounted and pulled their mounts behind the grassy ridges and promptly vanished. For an instant, Canyon could hear only the soft thud of their horses' hooves on the thick turf, and then nothing. Swallows and Canyon remained in the saddle and rode up onto a grassy knoll and pulled to a halt in plain sight of the approaching riders. As the crew rode closer, they dropped out of sight momentarily as they traversed a long swale. When they popped up again they were much closer and Canyon was able to make out clearly Lance Caulder riding well out in front of the others.

As soon as Caulder got to within fifty yards of Swallows and Canyon, he reined in and waited for his riders to catch up to him. Canyon counted twelve men in all. After a quick conference with his foreman, Caulder rode toward Canyon and Swallows, halting when he judged himself to be close enough to make himself heard without shouting. His riders did not move up with him. They sat their mounts alertly, watching.

"What is this, Swallows?" Caulder demanded. "How come you're sidin' with this here damn Yankee?"

"You didn't think I'd take *your* side, did you?"

"Maybe you don't understand, Jim. That sonofabitch beside you is fixin' to take me in for a hanging."

"So he tells me."

"And you're still siding him?"

"Yep. Be a right good thing you meetin' with a hangman. I got kin had to deal with your bushwhackers. You and Quantrill didn't leave them much when you got through with them. Except heartache."

"So that's why you been standin' off from me, is it?"

"That's why."

"Pity you didn't have the courage to brace me before this."

"Better late than never. I'll be glad to see you and your killers pull out—one way or the other. Take away some of the stink hangin' over this land. Do the air good. Freshen it up."

The insult was studied and ferocious—and its barb sank deep. Canyon saw Caulder flinch with fury and lean forward over his cantle like a cur dog straining on a leash. Back in Caulder's antebellum south such an insult would have meant a duel to obtain satisfaction. But that world was gone now, gone with the wind—or was it?

"I guess you just had to say your piece, Yankee lover," Lance snarled. "Well, now it's my turn."

"Is it?"

Swallows unholstered his Colt and sent a quick round into the air. Before the detonation's echo faded, the soft, rapid drumming of horse's hoofs sounded as Swallows's men swept up out of the tall grass and closed in on Caulder and his crew, their sidearms drawn and ready.

At the same time, Canyon drew his Henry from its scabbard and levered a fresh round into its chamber.

Glancing quickly about him at the enclosing circle of riders, Caulder snarled, "You sonofabitch, Swallows! You tricked us!"

Swallows smiled coldly. "Tell you what I'll do. I'll send a shot over your head. If you're not on your way by then, I'll just lower this here revolver and keep on firing."

"You ain't heard the last of this!" Caulder cried.

"I sincerely hope not."

Swallows pulled the trigger. The round seared the air over Lance Caulder's head, close enough for him to hear it. He flung his horse around and raced back through the ranks of his men, who wheeled their horses in turn and galloped after him.

Not long after, Canyon and Jim Swallows were relaxing on Jim's porch, seated on homemade wooden chairs. As Swallows told it, he was a relative latecomer to New Mexico Territory, having driven his herd of longhorns here from Texas directly after the war. Most of the other big ranchers had arrived earlier, he explained, their herds supplying much of the beef the Confederates needed so desperately—this despite the attempt by the New Mexico Volunteers, led by Kit Carson, to halt the traffic. Since Swallows himself had fought for the Confederate cause and been wounded in the Second Battle of Bull Run, he did not find fault with the actions of those cattlemen.

The wooden chairs they were occupying were covered with buffalo robes and, when Canyon commented on this, Swallows told him there was still a sizable herd on this plateau—along with more than a few Utes to hunt them come fall. As far as Swallows was concerned, both the buffalo and the Indians were welcome, though he knew well enough that before many more seasons passed both would vanish from this high, lush land.

"What about the Navahos?" Canyon asked.

"Kit Carson and his Utes took care of them back in '63. Burned their crops, their storehouses, drove them out of these parts."

Canyon nodded. He knew about the famous Colonel Kit Carson, all right—and what he and his Volunteers did later at Adobe Wells, standing off more than three thousand Comanches, while losing only twenty-five men.

"What about the Apaches?"

"Right now, they're busy with the Comanches, but there's talk of rounding them up and herding them onto reservations in the Arizona Territory."

"From what I hear, they're not likely to stay put for long."

Swallows nodded gloomily, then said, "The way I see it, what we have to do is replace the redskin's buffalo with our cattle. Once that's accomplished, we'll get no more trouble from the horse Indians."

"That's likely to be a long time from now."

"It's closer than you think. Some of my crew have already left to go buffalo hunting."

"Buffalo hunting?"

"For the skins—and the buffalo's tongues. There's a growing market for both items back East. Soon as they get that Transcontinental Railway built, you'll see how those herds melt, mark my words."

"The plains Indians won't stand still for that."

"That's right. They won't. Which means there'll be trouble. With the Comanches and Cheyenne, especially. But it won't matter. With that Sharps rifle these Buffalo skinners are using, they'll sweep the plains clear of buffalo before the redskins know what's happening."

Canyon could not help thinking Swallows was exaggerating. On his way out here, he had glimpsed two vast buffalo herds. There were so many buffalo in each one it took days for the buffalo to pass a given point. Might as well try to drain the ocean as wipe out the buffalo. But Canyon was in no mood to argue with his host. He liked the man and this high New Mexico spread of his. A jug of mescal sat between them on the porch. Twice already Canyon had sampled the fiery liquor and was content.

Abruptly, Swallows got up and began to pace.

"Seems to me, O'Grady, you'd have better luck bringing in an Apache chief than Lance Caulder. Knowing what I do about the man, I'd like nothing better than to see him cleared out of here. But he's the most powerful man in these parts, and with each ex-Confederate clan that shows up, he gets more powerful. Sometimes I think they're actually getting ready to try another assault on the Union. Maybe you'd better pull back a little."

"I didn't see you pulling back just now."

"I had a good-sized crew backing me. You're just one man."

"There's much truth in what you say, Jim," Canyon admitted ruefully. "The thing is, I came here thinking I'd be able to pick up Lance with a minimum of fuss."

"There's little chance of that now."

"I know. Seth Barton let the cat out of the bag. But I'm not going to back off now. I can't do that."

"I can understand how you feel." Swallows stopped pacing and slumped back down into his chair and hooked the jug up onto his shoulder. After a series of gulps, he wiped his mouth off with the back of his hand and passed the jug to Canyon.

"Why not spend the night," he asked Canyon. "You're more than welcome."

"I'd like to, but I've got other fish to fry. But thanks for the offer—and the hospitality."

Swallows's lean face creased into a grin. "Anytime at all, O'Grady. It has been a real pleasure. And I'm the one should be thanking you."

Canyon smiled.

The pleasure Swallows was talking about was the opportunity Canyon had provided for him to poke a stick in Lance Caulder's eye—an exercise Swallows had enjoyed immensely.

5

It was just before dusk when Canyon bid good-
bye to Swallows and rode back through the pass.
He was well into the timber, moving through
growing darkness, when he heard the first faint
pound of a rider coming up on him from behind.
He turned off the trace and pulled up in a clump
of aspen and waited for the rider to overtake him.
But he swung south before reaching him, the
pound of his horse's hoofs fading rapidly.

Something in the rider's urgency alerted Canyon. Any rider pushing his horse that hard
through such rough country with only the stars to
light the trail ahead of him meant trouble. Bad
trouble.

And the rider appeared to be heading for Steadman's Sun Ranch.

Canyon swung back down onto the trail, crossed
it and followed the lone horseman's dying echo into
the trees. Keeping a steady pace through the dim
files of timber was not easy. Close to half an hour
later, he felt the palomino growing slack under him
and decided he had better hold up some to give it
a rest. He was looking for a stream when he heard
the sullen, ominous pound of many hooves coming

from a trail in the timber below him. Whoever they were, they were pushing their mounts just as hard as that other ride.

Pulling up, Canyon lifted his head to listen as the dim thunder of hooves increased, reached a peak, then fell off rapidly to the south—going in the same direction as the rider Canyon was following. Starting up again, he followed the fading thunder of the riders as rapidly as he could. The palomino—obviously irritated at Canyon's insistence on going on—frequently slowed under him, shaking its head occasionally in protest. But Canyon urged it on without stint, the alarm he felt growing sharper the closer he got to the Steadman's place. It was more than alarm. It was a certainty when he passed the lone, blackened pine Helen had pointed out to him.

A moment later came the first faint rattle of gunfire, the sound borne on the cool night wind. There was no doubt where it came from. As he had feared: the Sun Ranch. He urged the flagging palomino to a faster pace. The firing was constant now, not heavy volleys, but a steady, determined pace—the way it would sound if dug-in forces were hunkered down and sending lead at a solid target.

Like a ranchhouse.

He broke out onto the timbered slope above the ranch. He charged down the slope, crossed the meadow and the road, and continued on up a gentle rise to the rear of the ranch buildings. Approaching the horse barn, he snatched his Henry from its scabbard and leaped from the nearly spent palomino. As the animal pulled up and trotted gratefully away into the night, Canyon scaled the corral fence and ran the remaining distance to the barn, entering through the rear.

He heard someone at one of windows firing a six-gun. The man was enjoying himself so hugely, he did not hear Canyon come up behind him. A powerful stench of raw whiskey clung to the gunman like a curse. Canyon raised his Colt over his head and brought it down squarely on top of the man's head, crushing the crown of his Stetson and spilling the fellow onto the hay-strewn floor. When the downed man stirred and tried to regain his feet, Canyon kicked him in the chops, sending him reeling senseless into a horse stall.

Canyon crouched down behind the window and saw a column of thick black smoke pulsing from the ranchhouse's rear kitchen window. As he watched the windows in the rear of the building blew out as the kitchen exploded in flames. The front of the house was not yet in flames, and from one of its windows came a desultory, useless return fire. The night riders, cloaked in darkness, were posted all about the yard, pouring a merciless, withering fire into the ranchhouse, apparently content simply to blaze away now at that now-shattered windows.

Lifting his Henry, Canyon picked out one shadowy figure by the porch corner. He rested his sight on a spot just behind the flash of the night rider's six-gun and squeezed off a shot. The man cried out and pitched forward. Levering swiftly, Canyon fired on two more attackers and by then found that he was a target. With slugs whining in through the barn's shattered window and punching holes in the barn's siding, Canyon clambered up into the loft and from the hay-loading doorway continued to pour fire down on the shadowy figures scuttling frantically about below him, his Henry growing warm with its steady employment.

By now, the flames billowing skyward were sending a garish pretense of daylight over the yard, giving the attackers less and less concealment. Abruptly someone shouted to the men, telling them to pull out. It was Lance Caulder. Canyon had no difficulty recognizing his harsh voice. Taking their wounded with them, Caulder's men bolted to their horses, mounted up and galloped off. Before they vanished into the night, Canyon managed to get a quick glimpse of Slim Winner—but saw no sign of Lance.

Canyon dropped to the ground and raced up the porch and into the burning ranchhouse. It felt as if he had charged into the open door of a furnace— which in truth he had. Shrouded in thick, choking coils of smoke just ahead of him, Helen was dragging her father's limp body toward him. Canyon lifted the injured man, flung him over his shoulder and, with Helen darting out ahead of him, carried the man from the blazing house.

＼ In the yard Helen turned suddenly, her eyes wide with concern. "Juan!" She cried. "He's still in there. He's been hit!"

Canyon put her father down just inside the barn's entrance, left them and darted back into the inferno. Peering through the smoke, he was just able to make out Juan's slumped figure in a corner. His eyes smarting fiercely from the thick smoke, Canyon slung the old man over his shoulder and ducked out of the house, nearly stumbling as he descended the front porch steps with his burden.

Just inside the barn, Helen was crouched down beside her father. As Canyon lowered Juan gently down beside Steadman, he glanced at Helen's father. A round had entered his chest just above his lungs, but the wounded man's eyes were open and Canyon saw in them a grim, angry determination to stay alive. He looked back at Juan and rested the back of his hand against the old man's neck artery. He found no pulse. He had rescued a dead man. He closed Juan's eyelids and threw a saddle blanket over him, then turned to Helen.

There were tears in her eyes. "Dead?"

Canyon nodded and looked quickly around, an angry frown on his face. "Where's the rest of your crew?"

"One of the men rode in and warned the crew what was up. They lit out. Juan was the only one stayed." She glanced over at his dead body. "I wish now he hadn't."

"I know it was Caulder and his bushwhackers," he told her. "But why?"

Steadman spoke up then, his voice barely audible. "He knew Helen and I warned you. This is a reminder—to the rest of the hill ranchers."

"So they'll steer clear of me."

It was Helen who answered. "Yes."

Canyon bent close to examine Helen's father. The man's eyes were closed, his breathing labored. Canyon didn't like how he sounded and realized the chest wound might very well prove fatal if they did not get the man to a doctor soon.

"You better bring your father into Placer

Town," he told Helen, "so Doc Sanderson can take a look at him."

"That quack?"

"He's all you got."

A sudden roar came from the burning ranchhouse, and Canyon stood up in the barn doorway to watch the fire finish its job. The ranchhouse's roof had already collapsed, filling the night sky with flaming embers. The walls vanished in the blaze and soon it was clear that the only thing that would remain upright would be the fieldstone chimney. Helen appeared in the doorway beside him. Canyon glanced at her. Tears rolled without shame down her cheeks as she watched the fiery destruction of what had once been her home.

"Come on," Canyon said, pushing her gently out of the doorway. "Don't look any more. You've got to think of your father now. Let me help you hitch up that team."

Eyes dull now with hurt and despair, Helen allowed Canyon to lead her back into the barn.

At the first light of dawn, Helen left with her father.

Canyon watched the flatbed wagon disappear down the road, then walked into the barn and turned his attention to the gunman still lying unconscious in the horse stall. He nudged him none too gently with his boot until the man stirred. Canyon stepped back as the man sat up groggily, both hands holding his aching head. There was a gash on the side of his chin where Canyon's boot had struck it. He still stank of rotgut and Canyon figured it was this as much as Canyon's boot that had kept him on ice this long.

Canyon bent over, grabbed the man's shirt front, and hauled him upright.

"Who the hell're you?" the fellow blustered.

"I'm the one kicked you in the head. That was Lance Caulder leading your bunch last night, wasn't it."

"Sure."

"Where's Lance?"

"How the hell would I know?"

"I think you know and I think you better tell me."

The man moistened dry lips and tried to pull free of Canyon's grasp. "What's in it for me if I tell you?"

"That's easy. I won't make you eat horseshit."

For a moment or two the man looked closely at Canyon, as if measuring Canyon's tenacity. Then he shrugged. "Lance rode north."

"That's not good enough," Canyon told him.

Canyon spun the man around and shoved him head first into a stall with such force the man went down on all-fours over a neat pile of horse manure. Canyon rested his right foot on the back of the fellow's neck and pressed downward. When the man's snout was only inches from the fragrant pile of horseshit, he struggled frantically, then blurted, "All right! All right! I'll tell you!"

Canyon eased slightly the pressure on the man's neck. "Let's have it."

"Lance is headin' for the other hill ranchers. This here's a warning to them. If they don't join

72

with him to track you down, they're all going the same way as the Sun Ranch."

"Which ranch is he headin' for first?"

"Sam Gills's place. The Lazy S."

Canyon stepped back. The Dixieland rider pushed himself back out of the stall, then got to his feet.

"Get on your horse and clear out of this country," Canyon told him. "And keep riding."

A moment later, Canyon watched the Dixieland gunslick ride out, heading south. Canyon had no confidence the man would continue in that direction, but that hardly mattered. He went for his horse. Jim Swallows had a right to know what was happening.

"My God, Canyon," Jim said, leaving the porch hurriedly. "How's Helen?"

Canyon dismounted and dropped his reins over the hitchrack. "She's as good as can be expected. But I'm not so sure about her father."

"Steadman?"

"He's been hit bad. High in the chest. Helen's taking him in to Placer Town to see the Doc."

"Juan's dead?"

Canyon nodded.

"And you say the Sun Ranch's been burnt out."

"The ranchhouse, anyway. And Steadman's riders are gone."

"That son of a bitch."

"Caulder's back to his old tricks, looks like. Once a bushwhacker, always a bushwhacker."

"What do you want me to do, Canyon?"

"Whatever pleases you the most. I'm going to warn Gills if I can get to his place soon enough—

and then the other hill ranchers. If you could throw in with us, it might tip the scales."

"I'll do it. Of course. But first, I want to ride into Placer Town. Check on how Helen and her father are."

"I can understand that."

"Then I'll get my men and ride north to join you at Gills's place. You sure you can find it?"

"I'll find it."

"Watch out for that bastard Caulder."

"You don't have to tell me that."

"Ride, then. I'll move out as soon as I can get my men together. Good luck, and keep your ass down."

"I'd like to water the palomino first."

"Of course. Is there anything else you need?"

"That'll be it."

"I'll join forces with you later at the Lazy S then."

Swallows hurried back into his ranchhouse. Canyon led the palomino over to the water trough in front of the barn.

Canyon was close to five miles into the timber beyond the pass, moving through growing darkness, when he heard the first faint pound of riders coming up on him from behind. He pulled into a clump of aspen and watched as the bunch of Dixieland riders—Karl Berdick in the lead—swept on north, the pound of their hooves fading rapidly.

Canyon waited until the sun vanished from the sky, then rode on, keeping to the north, riding through dim files of Douglas fir. Above the treetops, the sky was awash with stars, sending a faint patina of light through the branches onto the trail ahead of him. A cooling, pine-laden wind brushed his cheek gently. It was close to midnight when he made camp by a high, swift stream.

He woke at dawn and set out again, and by mid-afternoon found himself at the point of the vaulting range where it tilted up into sheer rock faces. He paused to look back at the timbered hills and valleys, the meadows and flats scattered between them like torn scraps of clothing, then turned back around in his saddle and peered up through the sparse timber at the rocky slope before him. Belle Summerfield had calculated that Sam Gills's ranch would be only a two-day ride beyond the Sun Ranch.

Maybe so, but Canyon doubted it.

She had also warned him that he would be traveling through steep, rough country—and that part he believed. With a fatalistic shrug, he nudged the palomino on up through the sparse timber. Before long he found himself following a faint trail around boulders and steep cliff faces that took him past small patches of snow. Warped and stunted conifers found a hold in narrow fissures in the rockfaces. A hardy grass Canyon had never seen before poked up through the meager, rocky soil. Sharp winds swept Canyon with the clean cold of the distant snow fields. By noon he was lost in this profound upland labyrinth of rock and great slashed canyons that twisted and fell, and tumbled and angled and doubled back. For a while it looked as if he would not be able to escape the ring of penning, snow-capped peaks.

At dusk he found a game trail to guide him and

soon rode into a tight flat valley with an icy stream snaking through it, and decided to make camp. He was surprised the next morning how well he had slept and by how ravenous he was. By full daylight he was on the trail again, a raw wind that smelled of rain beating in his face. It seemed to him as he traveled between these rugged, cold peaks that this range was endless, and that all he would ever see again would be these encircling mountain peaks shrouded in thunderheads.

Ravines gaped before him. He held to the crest of timbered ridges for as long as possible, then dropped into them, crossed over and rose to the next ridge, the sun dropping steadily in a cloudless sky. Near sunset, the trees opened before him, and he faced a creek running quickly over its stones. Beyond it, heavy timber clothed the slopes. He crossed the creek and nudged the palomino into the timber, then paused to look back and gaze up and down the creek. Only when he was satisfied he was alone, did he return to the water's edge and let the palomino satisfy its thirst. Then he moved back into the timber. A mile or so farther on he came to a trail looping stiffly back up the side of the mountain face blocking his path. Since there was no other way, he took it.

He rose steadily with the short switchback courses, higher and higher along the edge of the cliff as daylight slowly faded from the sky. He arrived at last to a leveling-off place, gave the timbered slope below him one last look, and kept himself moving on toward the peaks. It was not long before the trail brought his palomino to a complete standstill at the edge of a precipice running three hundred feet or more downward into a canyon whose bottom was already dim with night shadows.

The land was deceptive. He had marched out of one canyon to these heights, and now faced another canyon. Night wind began to flow off the peaks still looming above him, and as he peered into the canyon below him, he saw the tide of darkness slowly drown out its floor. A narrow game trail dropped along the face of the precipice, running lower and lower until he could no longer see its course.

There was undoubtedly a better way of moving off this ridge. One end of it was probably anchored against the peaks, providing him with a level route. But it was growing rapidly darker and he wanted a more sheltered spot for his camp. He urged the palomino down onto the trail. The cliffside was composed of old, weathered rock. The trail itself was no more than three or four feet wide, sometimes tightening against the cliff, causing Canyon's leg to scrape occasionally against it as he descended. The palomino, meanwhile, was both tired and doubtful of the trail and frequently stopped, so that Canyon had to use his heels to force it on. At times the trail pitched downward so steeply that the palomino's hoofs slid along the loose dirt and pebbles, and the farther the trail dropped, the blacker it became, until a smothering darkness settled over Canyon. There was nothing visible above him and nothing for him to see below the trail.

He had gone a hundred feet or so farther when the palomino stopped and refused to go on. Canyon bent forward over its neck and fixed his eyes on the ledge before him until he thought he saw the continuation of the trail. He urged the horse on again. The animal gathered its feet close together and began to proceed with infinite care, moving forward and down in tiny mincing shifts. Canyon felt his own shoulder brushing close against a solid face of rock as the palomino turned slowly until it had completely reversed its direction. Then it headed downward again with considerably more confidence.

Looking back and down, Canyon was only barely able to make out the turnaround the horse had sensed—and realized how completely his own eyes had betrayed him. It gave him pause and more than a twinge of uncertainty. But he was committed now to this descent and had no choice but to go on. Leaning back in the saddle to ease the animal's burden somewhat, he slackened the reins. He had no other course, he realized now, but to trust to the palomino's instinct.

The horse kept on slowly, steadily, stopping occasionally to blow, but keeping on—and all the while the darkness about Canyon grew so profound he felt as if he were descending into a soot-filled chimney. Then, without warning, the horse halted and made no effort to go on. Canyon waited a few moments, peering beyond the horse's flickering ears at the nothingness that yawned before them both. But the inky blackness swam like something substantial before his eyes as he fought to bring out of the gloom some image, some notion of what lay ahead. He gave this up at last and sat back in his saddle, content to wait for the horse to move. He waited a full two minutes, he judged.

Then, knowing that something stood in the way and that the palomino would go no farther, he dismounted and edged carefully past the horse, moving between it and the canyon wall—his hands holding tightly to the reins.

Once in front of the horse, he lit a match and held it out as far as he could. He saw ahead of him a fresh, damp landslide of rock and soil sitting on the trail, blocking it completely. A wet spot in the cliff wall just above the ledge had collapsed onto the trail, but the slide was a recent one and not yet packed firm. The match winked out. He got down on his hands and knees and inched forward to the slide and, running his hands shovel-like into the dirt and other debris, began throwing it off the ledge into the void below him. As he worked, he could barely hear the rocks and clumps of soil coming to rest on the canyon floor, so far below him was it.

It took him at least a half hour to clear away the rocks, boulders, and other debris and, when he had finished, his hands were raw. He caught up the horse's reins and led it cautiously forward. Fifty feet farther on brought him to still another uncertain spot. He got down once more on his hands and knees, probing into the blackness ahead of him with his hands, and found he had come to another sharp turnaround. He stood up and let the horse take its time following after him as he made the turn and continued the descent on foot.

Soon afterwards, he could hear the sound of water flowing through the canyon far below him and, not long after that, its cold dampness began to reach him. He kept on and the dampness increased, as did the sound of the rushing water. He had been on this descent for what seemed an interminable time, and was anxious to put it behind him. But he forced himself to move on only with the greatest caution, walking with a short forward step as he led the palomino, gradually becoming more sure of himself as the canyon floor appeared nearer.

The horse halted. He saw no reason for it and tugged on the horse impatiently. When he got it moving again, he stepped forward, but his foot found nothing solid to plant on. Losing his balance, he plunged forward into emptiness. His grip tightened convulsively on the reins and as he swung forward, one foot still on the trail, his sudden weight caught the horse by surprise and it flung its head up and stepped back. Clinging to the reins, Canyon swung outward into space, his other foot slipping off the trail. His chest slammed into the side of the cliff face.

Near panic, the spooked palomino shied backward, dragging Canyon along the sharp edge of the trail, the rocks sawing violently at his ribs. He managed to hook one elbow over the ledge, then the other and thus anchored, let go the reins and boosted himself back up onto the trail. He lay flat on the ground a moment, catching his breath and appreciating the feel of solid ground under him, then rolled over and sat upright. He glanced at the palomino. In the inky blackness he could catch only the gleam of its trembling flanks.

"Thanks, horse," he told it. "You did just fine." The palomino stamped its front feet and shook its head, the jingling of its bit echoing brightly in the canyon.

"No need to get carried away," Canyon told it, grinning.

He got up and walked with infinite care to the break in the trail. He lit another match, its feeble flame lost in the fathomless darkness looming beyond him. But before the match went out, he glimpsed the trail again beyond the gulf. He pulled back, found a couple of small rocks, and threw the first one at least three feet ahead of him. It bounced once, then dropped into the void below the trail. He sent the second rock after the first one, throwing this one harder. It bounced on the trail on the other side of the gap, confirming Canyon's judgment that it was not less than six feet away.

He sat back then, struck another match and held it cupped in his hands close against the cliff wall. This time he saw enough before the match guttered out to give him hope. Only the outer margin of the trail was gone. The inner portion hugging the wall remained intact. This left only a dangerously narrow path for them, but one that might— with some luck—be negotiable for both him and the palomino.

He rose and tested the ledge's footing, running his hands along the face of the cliff to give himself direction. His foot struck a rock large enough to cause trouble. He threw it off the trail, then approached the horse, took off its saddle, and carried it across the break, his cheek resting against the cool wall of rock as he inched along. He dumped the saddle onto the trail, returned to the horse, caught up its reins, and led the animal forward, grasping the extreme end of the reins. Halfway out onto the narrow remnant of the trail, he turned and yanked gently on the reins, calling softly to the horse as he did so. It had already proven itself to be a sure-footed brute, but it was now also a very wary one as well, and when it came to the break, it halted.

Canyon returned to the palomino, inched past its neck, and used the pressure of his body to shift the animal close to the wall. Then he moved out ahead of it and yanked on the reins again. This time the horse took a firm step forward onto the narrow strip, and then another. As soon as it was beyond the break, Canyon dropped the reins to allow the horse to lower its head and sniff the trail for itself. The horse thrust its muzzle downward, breathing and snorting tentatively at the ledge under its feet. Canyon felt it place a wary forefoot down on it, hesitate a moment, then advance the other front foot. He heard its flanks scraping along the rock face. Speaking gently to the palomino, he reached out to take its reins.

Suddenly the horse's hind foot, too close to the edge, slid off, and the horse made a quick lunge that carried it all the way across to firm ground, the surge catching Canyon by surprise. Struck in the chest, he was flung backward. He stumbled and fell, his hand striking the ledge, then slipping off it. He fought for a desperate moment to keep his balance and just managed to prevent himself from tumbling off into space.

The horse snuffling over him, Canyon inched back, then got to his feet, reached over for the saddle and slapped it back onto the horse and made a loose tie. A cold wind scoured through the canyon, but his face was sticky with the sweat that streamed down his face. He took up the reins and led the palomino on, taking each step with infinite caution. By this time he was completely exhausted—as much from the natural weariness caused by a full day's ride as by the accumulating tension of this excruciating descent.

He reached the canyon floor without further incident, the trail playing out through gravel and chunks of rock. Soon he could feel as well as hear the river thundering in the darkness before him. He kept on until he reached the river and caught the moon's dim glow on its black, glassy surface. The gravel on the bank river churned under his feet. The palomino stumbled and stopped, as worn out as Canyon.

He kept on, nevertheless, until he reached a grassy spot. Here Canyon unsaddled the horse again and hobbled it. Then he found a grassy knoll and put down his soogan. Once inside it, he rested his head back against his saddle, closed his eyes, and was almost instantly asleep. What woke him close to dawn was a stone grinding with seemingly malignant intent into his back. He rolled off it and blinked the grit out of his eyes and looked up at the cliff side dimly visible before him. The sky brightened, and he stood up, stretched, then walked over to the bank of the creek and relieved himself, after which he rolled up his bedding and saddled up the palomino.

He nooned on a ridge, followed another canyon through the afternoon, and a couple of hours or so before dusk dismounted by the creek running through it. He was letting the palomino drink its fill when he glanced up at the canyon rim and saw someone standing on it. Even as Canyon reached for his Henry, the man brought up his own rifle—it had the look of a Henry or one of those new Winchester .44's—and fired. The round whined off a boulder less than a foot from him. The palomino flung up its head at the sound, but Canyon clung to the reins and swiftly mounted up. A second round exploded the gravel at its feet. Canyon kept the horse from rearing in panic, clapped his heels to it, and rode on down the canyon. A huge boulder loomed before him. As he veered around it, a third round smacked off its surface. He kept going, his head bent low over the horse's neck and saw ahead of him a long, low log shack huddled close under the canyon wall. He veered toward it and when he reached it, flung himself to the ground, and hauled the horse after him into it.

Inside it, he found empty bunk frames against the walls. The flooring was hard-packed dirt, and early morning sunlight gleamed through cracks in the roof. Canyon stepped back into the doorway. On the canyon rim above, the lone rifleman spilled off his mount, swung up his rifle, and pumped a series of rifle shots methodically through the flimsy shake roof. Canyon pulled the horse after him through the length of the ramshackle building to a far corner that offered a little more protection from the fusilade.

The firing ceased for a moment as the rifleman reloaded. Canyon knew that if he stayed where he was, a chance shot would sooner or later reach him or cripple the palomino. Judging from the pattern of bullet holes on the floor, it was clear to Canyon that the marksman intended to rake the bunkhouse from one end to the other.

Canyon peered out one shattered window. On the canyon rim the rifleman swung his rifle's bore in Canyon's direction and squeezed off a shot. Canyon ducked back, but not before he glimpsed a covey of horsemen—Lance Caulder at its head—riding up to join the rifleman. A second or two later the rest of the riders opened up a deadly fusilade, the hot lead crashing down through the shake roof and sending clods of dirt flying up from the floor. Canyon caught the palomino's reins in his left hand, slapped the horse out through the door, mounting up as it bolted from the shack. He was twenty feet from it, galloping along the strip of meadow along the creek, when the fire from the canyon rim swung after them.

The range was two hundred feet or more, yet even so the rifle fire came uncomfortably close. He veered in closer to the cliff wall, occasionally scraping it as he rode, then looked back and up and saw one man leaning out from the rim, his rifle trained on him. When the shot came, the round missed Canyon by three or four yards, exploding the gravel just in front of the palomino's plunging hoofs. He kept going and turned with the cliff's gradual bend and when again he looked back he found himself sheltered from further fire.

He reined in then to get his bearings. The canyon's wall made a slow turn and opened onto a wide swath of open country, while the wall on the other side remained sheer as far as he could see.

Across the stream, a ridge's timbered shoulders rose steeply until it came hard against the flanks of a rugged escarpment that lifted to a series of jagged peaks. He turned the palomino and charged from the cover of the canyon wall and galloped full tilt into the stream. As the firing resumed behind him, he set the horse upstream for better footing, the surging water sometimes reaching as high as the palomino's chest. Above the rush of the water, Canyon heard Caulder and his men opening up on him again, the sound of their gunfire a faint popping. Spent rounds plunged into the stream with a faint, gurgling sound.

Canyon turned the palomino. It left the stream and charged across the narrow beach toward the timbered slope. Once he gained the shelter of the pines, he looked back and saw that, as he had already suspected, Lance Caulder and his men were clearly visible against the side of the cliff, moving down it its steep side in single file. He counted at least twelve men, spaced out and moving with great caution as they descended. Canyon estimated that in another five minutes the outfit would reach the canyon floor and charge across the stream in hot pursuit.

Canyon turned his palomino and rode on into the timber, the needle-carpeted slope lifting steadily under him. In what he judged to be something less than five miles into the timber, he came to a broad upland meadow and charged across it. Once he reached the timber beyond it, he dismounted and snaked his Henry from its scabbard and slapped the palomino's flank, sending it on up the slope ahead of him. He was pretty goddamn sick of running before Lance Caulder's hot lead and was looking forward to sending some of his own back at the bastard. He found a fallen log and made himself comfortable behind it.

As soon as the first pursuing rider charged from the timber, Canyon lifted the Henry to his shoulder and tracked him. Behind this one, in rapid succession, a hard-driving string of riders emerged from the timber. Canyon waited to see if the lead rider was Lance Caulder, and when he got close enough for him to see that it wasn't, Canyon swore in frustration and let his finger tighten about the trigger. The Henry's stock slammed his shoulder, the sharp detonation rolling across the meadow.

The rider yanked back on his mount's reins and tumbled off the horse, dragging it violently to one side. The rider landed hard, rolled over once, then lay still. The other riders coming up from behind spilled to a halt around the downed man. Two of them flung themselves from their horses, some to examine the downed rider, others to take cover. Canyon turned and raced back up the slope to his horse. Vaulting into the saddle, he kicked the horse on up through the timber. The horse found the footing tough going, but tugged valiantly, doggedly, upward over some of the most difficult ground Canyon had ever seen.

As the slope became almost vertical, he found he had no recourse but to dismount and lead the palomino. He broke through the nearly impenetrable vine undergrowth for it, circled great masses of fallen rock and soil, and skirted windfalls lying breast high before him. The horse came patiently after him, now and then clearing a gully with a lunge that brought the animal hard against Canyon, at one time pushing him to the ground. The grade, meanwhile, tilted upward with ruthless persistence until it became so difficult for the horse to keep its footing on the grade that only Canyon's added weight on the bridle kept the animal from sliding back down.

It went on like this for close to an hour until at last Canyon broke from the timber onto a long, grassy benchland. He pulled up wearily and let his gaze sweep its length. Steep peaks reared skyward all around and, at the end of the benchland, perched high on a bluff amidst a crown of Douglas fir, he saw a massive log house.

Canyon had reached the Lazy S ranch.

6

Canyon mounted up and rode the length of the benchland, then cut diagonally up onto the bluff. Screened by the fir, he approached the log house and, the closer he got, the more impressed he became. The main house was a solidly constructed two-story affair with shingle roofing and a rough, but sturdy porch fronting it. The roof of the porch served as the floor for the second-story balcony, French doors opening onto it, a sturdy white railing encompassing it. A huge horse barn and a smaller barn alongside it were tucked in among the fir behind the house. Chicken houses and pig pens, a bunkhouse, a cookhouse, a tool shed, and a smithy's shack made up the remainder of the ranch's outbuildings. It was a sizable ranch—and a prosperous one, judging from what Canyon could make out.

He pulled up and studied the ranch through the trees. How far behind him Caulder and his riders were he had no idea; there had been no sign of them since he reached the benchland. But they would be showing up soon enough, he had no doubt.

Canyon found himself frowning as an uneasy,

prickly sensation fell over him. The log mansion was as quiet as a mausoleum. Where the hell was everybody? Keeping in the timber, he urged the palomino to within hailing distance of the big house.

"Hello, the house!" he called.

There was no response. He called out again, then looked about the ranch compound and saw nothing out of order, no sign of trouble—except for the uncanny absence of any ranch hands. An outfit this large and this prosperous had to have a pretty large and powerful force of riders.

He dismounted slowly and stood quietly beside the palomino.

"All right," a heavy, guarded voice behind him said. "Just stay right where you are, mister."

Canyon heard the chink of spurs as a boot came down on the ground and then the blowing of a horse. The soft thunder of other hoofs came then and from all sides through the trees came the riders Canyon had guessed had to be about.

A man walked past Canyon with a gun in his hand, swinging it idly at his side. Holstering the gun in a flapped, black leather Navy holster, he turned to look at Canyon—a heavy-set man in his early forties with a tough, leathery face. It was bleak now with a weariness that seemed bone-deep.

"You Sam Gills?" Canyon asked.

"Who's askin'?"

Glancing at the riders sitting their mounts on all sides of him, Canyon told Gills.

"Canyon O'Grady, is it?"

"That's right."

"Well, I'm Sam Gills, and this here is my crew. You mind tellin' me what in the hell you're doin' up here?"

"I'm after Lance Caulder."

"And I'm goin' to rope the moon. What're you talkin' about, mister?"

"Caulder's a man wanted for his crimes during the war."

"I thought the war was over."

"Not for some people."

"Ain't that the truth." Gills took a deep breath. "So you're the one stirred up this hornet's nest, sent Caulder on the warpath. Been wonderin' when you'd show up."

With a wave of his hand, Gills sent his men back into the timber. They melted away like ghosts, their glances back at Canyon cold and unfriendly. They had evidently just finished a hard ride and blamed him for it.

"Come up on to the porch, Canyon," Gills said, "and set a spell. We got some talkin' to do."

As soon as they mounted the porch, a tall, mournful fellow in a short apron appeared from within the big house, cups and a coffee pot in his hand, as if he had been hidden away for just this moment. He put the coffee pot and the cups down on a table on the porch, then hustled back into the house for the cream and honey. Canyon and Gills sat down at the table.

"We heard gunfire—then saw you comin'," said Gills, by way of explanation. "So me and my men rode back and Cookie kept his ass down inside the house. Didn't know but what you might be some kind of trick—a diversion, maybe."

"I assume you've already run afoul of Lance Caulder. I rode up here to warn you."

"Much obliged, but your warning comes a bit late. Lance has already burnt out the Hatchet—the next outfit over—and taken their cattle and a good deal of mine while he was at it. He rode up here as bold as brass and told me I was through in this country as well. Some action pulled him and his men off, but the sonofabitch will be back."

"That action was me, more than likely."

"How so?"

"One of his men caught sight of me. I took refuge in a line shack, but not for long."

"That's my line shack. You get in any licks?"

"One man I'm sure of, but that's all."

"Well, they'll be after driving their rustled cattle to market now. Lucky you happened along, after all. Saved a good deal of my herd, looks like."

"How many men you got?" Canyon asked, pouring the cream into his coffee.

"Seven."

"That's not half enough."

"Tell me something I don't know."

"You got help coming. Jim Swallows and his crew are on the way. Swallows will join forces with you to cut the odds some."

"Jim Swallows? The Box J?"

"That's what I rode up here to tell you. When Caulder burnt out the Sun Ranch, Swallows decided to throw in with you and the other ranchers."

"Caulder burnt out the Sun Ranch, you say?"

"Yes."

Gills shook his head. "No wonder Swallow's

making this move then. He's sweet on Helen Steadman. Besides that, him and Caulder's been at each other's throats for some time now. What more can you tell me? Is the Sun Ranch finished?"

"Just about. The ranchhouse is gone and so is the crew. Helen's father is in poor shape. He took a slug in the chest. Helen's taken him to Placer City."

"A fat lot of good that will do. But at least she's all right." He sipped his coffee thoughtfully. "With Swallow's men at our back we can make Caulder think twice now, but that won't stop him. He's got the other big ranchers, the rest of his Confederate bushwhackers to swell his ranks. They've been filling up this land—on his invite. They want this land all to themselves, and there ain't much to stop them. But I'm surprised at Swallows, throwing in with us poor white trash now—no matter how much he hates Caulder. He could live to regret it."

"Maybe I should go after Caulder."

"All by your lonesome?"

"I don't work well as part of an army. You said he's off selling his cattle. You mean he's taken the stolen herd to Silver Creek?"

"Not yet. He's got it hid up here somewhere. I know that for sure. But he's probably gone there to set up a deal."

"You mean you know where he's driven the cattle he's rustled."

"I mean I got a pretty good idea, but he's got enough men to hold of anyone who might want to take them cows back."

Canyon considered a moment. Then he finished

the coffee and cleared his throat. "I heard tell you hill ranchers have been maybe picking off a few cattle yourselves."

" 'Course we have. How do you think we got our herds started? But that don't mean Lance has to wipe us all out."

"And Hatchet—that other ranch he burnt out. Was Hatchet rustling cattle, too?"

Gills face went grim. "I got to admit it. Hatchet got greedy."

"Then you might say Hatchet got what it deserved."

"You can say that, but I won't."

"Anyway, this is not all black and white."

"What in life is, mister?"

"I also heard you were the leader of the hill ranchers, the one behind most of the rustling."

"Whoever told you that gave me more credit than I deserve."

"Belle Summerfield."

Gills chuckled. "'Well, now," he said, smiling. "I ain't goin' to say nothin' against that woman. I owe her too many favors."

"Me, too."

"So now it's a range war—and it looks like you're the fuse that set it off, Mister O'Grady."

"I still want Lance Caulder."

"He's more than likely at Silver Creek, or on his way there now, setting up buyers for the cattle he's just rustled."

"Guess that's where I'll be heading, then."

By noon of the next day, Canyon was once again deep in a tortured upland of windswept ridges and slashed canyons. And then he found something to guide him, a wide trail pounded out of the thin soil by the feet of countless hooves. Following it, he could see where the cattle had been hazed through tight defiles, leaving tufts of hair wedged into cracks in the walls. In his mind's eye he could see the steers milling frantically as they were pushed along, the air filled with dust and the sound of ropes smacking hides.

Once, where the shale-littered trail threaded the edge of a deep gorge, Canyon saw far below him a steer's carcass not yet picked clean by the buzzards. He dismounted and climbed down to where the steer lay across the stream, a little bloated. On the left hip, which was uppermost, Canyon saw where a generous patch of the hide had been cut out, the brand along with it. It didn't matter who the rustlers were—Sam Gills or Caulder—this was the route they took to Silver Creek.

Canyon climbed back up to the palomino and continued on. By mid-afternoon he came to a narrow valley that widened out between sheer cliffs. There was only a little grass on its floor and a stream that ran its course hard against one wall. He circled the flat and found the remains of a recent campfire, built on the dead, blackened core of countless other fires. He kept on and when night came picked a sheltered spot off the trail and made camp.

By midafternoon of the next day, as he traversed a long, barren plateau, he found himself leaning back in his saddle and realized he was traveling downslope. Soon, poking through the gray mists below him, he saw the tops of thin pines.

Before long he was riding through fragrant timber. At first he could see only a widening gap in the cloud-shrouded mountains, but as he rode on he glimpsed below him a dark, wide valley folded in between the peaks. He kept on, still following the dim cattle trail, until he reached the valley floor. There, the trail merged with others and soon became lost among them.

He followed the heavily traveled trace, came soon enough onto a deeply rutted road, and before long he found himself having to give way to huge ore wagons hauled by eight- and, in some cases, ten-horse teams. By then he was following along the bank of a wide, rapid stream.

Not one of the crew on the huge ore wagons that rumbled past O'Grady paid the slightest attention to him, and he took this to mean that riders from the other side of the range were no strangers to this land. He kept on and, where the valley narrowed, found Silver Creek. It was a rough, unpainted settlement of raw buildings and board shacks fronting a wide street fetlock-deep in mud. The place was very busy. The heavy ore wagons had churned the streets into barely navigable swamps, the mud-holes axle deep in spots. The drivers of the ore wagons uttered fierce and terrible imprecations at those foolish enough to drive buckboards and other frail rigs before them. Meanwhile, the early-morning mist had dissolved into a steady, miserable rain, while the men and the few women thronging the sidewalks did their best to ignore it as they went about their business.

Canyon worked his way down the jammed street to the livery stable where he gave his palomino over to a boy for graining. Leaving his gear above the stall he had rented, he left the livery and joined the crowd of miners and roustabouts moving along the board walks. Canyon saw mule skinners, prospectors, gamblers, promoters of all sorts, and an unusual preponderance of cold-eyed gunslicks, their hips agleam with well-oiled six-guns—and not a few of these men wore remnants of their Confederate gray uniforms.

Pausing under a general store's wooden awning, Canyon looked about to get his bearings. The steady din around him was familiar enough, but Canyon did not like the feel of the town. It made him edgy. The inhabitants of Silver Creek made an unholy mix. Since Silver Creek was both a mining and a border town, it had become a perfect place to draw the get-rich-quick schemers on the one hand, desperadoes and gunslicks on the other. Belle Summerfield was right. This was a perfect place to bring rustled cattle.

Canyon caught sight of what appeared to be the biggest and gaudiest saloon in town. It was called the Bonanza. He left the awning's protection and slogged through the rain to the saloon, mounted the steps, and shouldered his way through the batwings. It was still early in the afternoon, but the place was crowded, the air vibrant with the loud, steady hum of men's voices, the clink of poker chips, the rattle of tumbling dice. Along the right wall was the bar, an ornate, heavy affair of thick, highly polished mahogany, a bar-length mirror behind it. Canyon noted how the glasses had been stacked in front of the mirror to hide the ragged bullet holes that had been punched through it. He reached the bar and looked around. All the gambling tables—poker, monte, faro—were doing a brisk business. He ordered whiskey from the barkeep.

As the barkeep poured, Canyon told him that a man might have left word for him. He would be wanting to sell a herd he'd be bringing in soon."

"Who're you?" the barkeep asked.

"O'Grady. Canyon O'Grady."

"Where you from?"

Canyon smiled. "You'd not be knowing the place. Any word?"

The barkeep, as Canyon had hoped he would, consulted with the other three bartenders. Each man looked toward Canyon and then shook their heads emphatically. Unsatisfied, the barkeep called for the swamper, who was soon passing among the percentage girls, asking the same question.

Canyon waited, the whiskey warming his insides, helping slightly to ward off the close, fetid smell of unwashed men and sweaty feet. At the far end of the bar the saloon opened up into a larger room, where most of the percentage girls were seated at tables with the patrons. From there, steps led upstairs to the girls' cribs. A girl was moving up the stairs with her john, her hand poked down inside the front of his pants. Canyon turned his head idly to watch the piano player flailing away at his upright. The piano was dismally out of tune, but in the general tumult no one noticed or cared.

A voice behind him said, "Are you O'Grady?"

He turned. One of the bar girls was looking up at him, her pale face as hard as marble. Her dress was black, cheap, clinging voluptuously to her young, lush body.

"Yes," Canyon said.

"Buy me a drink so we can take a table in back."

Canyon ordered a drink for her and followed her to a table in the corner. She sat down first and tipped her head at him as he sat down across from her.

"You a cattle buyer?"

"Do you have some to sell?"

"Someone I know does."

"He got a name?"

She was studying Canyon with coldly appraising eyes, and finally she said quietly. "Caulder. Lance Caulder."

"Where is he?"

"Upstairs with a gun trained on both of us." She smiled slightly, coldly. "He saw you come in. You're supposed to go up there with me."

"I'll bet you weren't supposed to tell me that part—about Caulder and the gun, I mean."

"You're right. I wasn't."

"Why did you?"

"I'm a fool, I guess."

"That the only reason?"

She tossed her hair defiantly, her dark eyes exploding with malice. "I hate that son of a bitch, Lance Caulder—and the swine he runs with."

Canyon had taken the bottle to the table. He poured himself another shot of the whiskey. "What's your name?"

"Teresa. Tionetta is my real name. I am Italian, but they want me to be Mexican; so, here, I am Mexican."

"What shall I call you?"

She shrugged. "Call me Teresa. I will answer to it."

"Is Lance alone up there?"

"His foreman is with him. A man called Karl Berdick."

"I've heard the name, but I don't think I ever met the man. What's he look like?"

"He is a meat head, that one. He has big shoulders and a big belly and his eyes are too close together."

"That's the only one with Lance?"

"The other men who rode in with him have returned to get the herd he is selling."

"He saw me from the balcony, did he?"

"He was with me. One of the girls told him a buyer named O'Grady was looking for cattle. He left my room and saw you. Then he told me to come down here and bring you up to him."

"How much time did he give you?"

She shrugged. "Not much. I think maybe now you better finish your drink."

"And go up there with you?"

"He said he will kill me if I don' get you upstairs pronto."

Canyon finished his drink and stoppered the bottle. His creaky ruse had worked well enough—maybe too well. He glanced at her covertly.

"Tell me where he is right now. Precisely."

"Behind you on the balcony. Almos' directly overhead."

"His gun is unholstered?"

"He is holding it at his side."

Canyon glanced around. The saloon was as noisy

as ever, the faro table busy, the clink of poker chips filling the air, the piano still tinkling out of tune. But all three barkeeps were keeping a wary eye on him, he realized and, as Canyon watched, one of them glanced nervously up at the balcony. Canyon's good sense told him that Lance Caulder had the advantage on him this time and that maybe he should leave the saloon and wait for another chance to brace Caulder. But if he cleared out of the saloon, that would tell Caulder that Teresa had warned him. There was no telling how a man like Lance Caulder would retaliate. Whatever he did to her, it would not be pretty.

"I think it's time we went upstairs." Canyon said to Teresa as he got to his feet. "Act casual. Take my arm and lean on it as you steer me toward the stairway."

She got up and thrust her hand through the crook in his arm. He lifted his bottle from the table, and then they headed for the stairs. Teresa played her part well, leaning her head against his shoulder as they mounted the stairs while he apparently kept his attention focused entirely on her.

When they reached the balcony, Teresa guided his steps toward her crib, chatting softly with him—only her eyes revealing the tension she felt. Canyon saw no sign of Lance, but that did not surprise him. When Lance saw Canyon start for the stairs with Teresa, he had undoubtedly slipped into her crib to wait for him. Teresa stopped and reached for her doorknob. Before she could turn it, the door swung back. A grinning Lance Caulder was standing in the doorway, his revolver leveled on Canyon. Beside him stood Karl Berdick, the big man matching Teresa's unflattering description perfectly.

As if he were furious with Teresa for tricking him, Canyon swore and flung the girl to one side. As she stumbled back down the hallway, Lance looked past Canyon at her.

"You did fine, bitch," he told her. "Now get your hot ass downstairs and keep your mouth shut."

Teresa turned about and scampered for the stairs. When she reached them and started down, Canyon noticed a sudden hush from the saloon below as the piano's tinkle abruptly ceased. Caulder reached out and hauled Canyon into the crib and slammed the door behind him. Then he turned to smile at Berdick, his yellow teeth gleaming in his grimy, unshaven face.

"Look what we got here, Karl," he drawled. "We just finished bustin' our ass to ride him down, and then he walks right in here like a lamb to slaughter."

Covering Canyon carefully with his six-gun, Lance stepped closer and withdrew O'Grady's Colt from his holster. Then he stepped back, waggling his gun at Canyon.

"Now you all just git over by the window, O'Grady."

Canyon walked past the two men. Teresa's crib was little more than a long closet with a single window at the end of it looking out over the back alley. There was barely enough room in it for the girl's cot. As Canyon passed Lance, he saw the man reach down for a pillow, what he would need, Canyon realized, to muffle the crack of his revolver. Earlier, when he had mounted the stairs, he had shoved the whiskey bottle down between his belt and the small of his back. He reached back for it now and with all the force he could muster, shattered it on the side of Lance's head. Lance pitched forward across the cot, the top of his skull crunching into the wall.

Berdick reached out for him. Canyon stepped neatly to one side, grabbed the foreman's shirt collar, then ran him headlong toward the window. The hulking brute went through it head down, his massive shoulders sending glass and window sash flying. As his boots vanished from sight, he uttered a short, startled cry. Canyon poked his head out through the shattered window and peered down. It was still raining, the rutted back alley gleaming with puddles. Berdick had landed on his back in one of them, and as Canyon watched, the big foreman rolled over once, then collapsed facedown in the muck.

Canyon left the window to see to Lance Caulder. The man was twisting slowly on the cot, groaning. Canyon took his Colt back from him, then rolled Caulder over and aroused with a smart slap on both his cheeks. Lance sat up groggily. Canyon thrust the barrel of his Colt under his chin.

"Get up, Lance."

Blinking woozily, Caulder got to his feet.

With the barrel of his Colt, Canyon nudged Lance toward the door, leaned past him and opened it. Then he shoved Lance out onto the balcony. As they started for the stairs, a large, excited crowd swarmed up the stairway, two men in the lead, their sidearms in their hands. The older and shorter one was a middle-aged man in black trousers, half boots and Stetson. His partner was swarthy and wore a slicker shiny with rain.

"What're you doin' with Lance, mister?" the older man asked.

"Who are you?"

"Yancy Brothers. Ah'm the town marshal. This here's mah deputy, Sonny Colson."

"My name's O'Grady," Canyon told them. "Get out of my way. This is not your concern."

"He's a Yankee bounty hunter, Yancy," Lance said bitterly. "He thinks he's goin' to take me back to Washington."

Brothers looked Canyon up and down. "Does, he now?" he drawled, his accent almost as thick as Lance Caulder's. "You know anything about that man just landed in the alley?" he asked Canyon.

"He came after me," Canyon said. "I was defending myself."

Brothers chuckled. "Then it *was* you sent him out through that window?"

"I had no choice. Now get out of my way."

"You mean I should get out of your way because you're on official Yankee business."

"If you want to put it that way."

Brothers said quietly, "Well, you ain't takin' Lance Caulder nowhere, mister—not less'n you got a warrant. You got one?"

Canyon took a weary breath. "No," he said.

"In that case, you Yankee son of a bitch, I'm takin' you in to stand trial."

"I told you I was acting in self-defense."

"Then you ain't got nothin' to worry about."

As Brothers spoke, his deputy shifted slightly to one side, his eyes cold, the six-gun in his hand steadying. Canyon was facing not one but two gun-slicks, he realized, both perfectly willing to end matters on the spot—if that was what it took. He slowly lowered his Colt. Lance ducked past him, shoved through the onlookers crowding the balcony, and vanished down the stairs. Brothers stepped forward and took the gun out of Canyon's hand and stuck it into his belt, then stepped back.

"Okay, O'Grady. Let's take a trip."

Canyon allowed the two lawmen to escort him out of the saloon and down the street through the pounding rain to the town marshal's office. Once inside, Brothers escorted Canyon through a door and down a narrow corridor. At the end of it, he shoved Canyon into a cell, slammed the barred door shut, and locked it.

"What's the charge, marshal?" Canyon demanded. "Assault?"

"Murder."

"You must be out of your head."

"Karl Berdick's dead. Looks like you broke the poor son of a bitch's neck—and you already admitted you was the one tossed him through that window."

"Damn you, Brothers. I told you. I was only defending myself."

"You can explain all that at the trial."

"This is a frame, Brothers. I saw Berdick move after he landed. He didn't have any broken neck—not unless you broke it for him."

"You callin' me a liar?"

"I am."

Brothers unlocked the cell door, pulled it open, and strode into it. Before Canyon could fling up his arm to defend himself, the lawman brought down the barrel of his six-gun. The crushing blow caused lights to explode deep within Canyon's skull. His knees turned to rope. He was unconscious before his knees hit the floor.

7

When Canyon came to his senses, he found himself still on the floor, the moon's light streaming in through a barred window. He sat up at once and immediately wished he hadn't. His head rocked wildly. Probing the top of his skull gingerly, his fingers found a sizable bump where the gunbarrel had struck him. But there was no break. He would live, he decided ruefully.

He picked up his hat and walked over to the door and peered through the bars. He saw only an empty corridor, a single window at one end, a door to the town marshal's office at the other. There were four other cells besides his, each one empty. He sat down on the bunk, the moonlight pouring over his shoulder, his thoughts chasing each other like a dog chasing its tail. Canyon did not believe for an instant that Karl Berdick had broken his neck in that fall. Canyon was sitting in this cell to give Caulder the time he needed to go back for his riders—and the rustled cattle he was peddling.

He heard the door at the end of the corridor open, then light footsteps hurrying toward his cell. He was standing at the bars, peering out, when Teresa appeared in front of him.

"You're in real trouble, Mr. O'Grady."

"That's not news to me, Teresa. Did you bring a hacksaw blade?"

"I'm serious! They're going to lynch you. I heard the men talking in the saloon. They're getting themselves tanked up to come down here and lynch you for Karl Berdick's murder."

"You mean he *is* dead?"

"Oh, my, I don' know. Nobody knows—or cares."

"You're right, Teresa. Any excuse—good, bad or indifferent—will do. Maybe you better help me get out of here."

She looked at him shrewdly, calculatingly. "All right, Mr. O'Grady. Why should I help you?"

"Because I'm innocent. I didn't kill anyone—and you and the rest of the townsmen know it."

"That's not enough of a reason—not for me. I've seen plenty of innocent men get shot down in cold blood in this town."

"I see. You want to know what's in it for you."

She moistened her lips nervously. "Yes."

"What do you want?"

"I want you to take me from this hellhole."

"That's crazy. If I get out of this mess, I'll be doing some hard riding. You'll only slow me down."

"I know how to ride—and shoot, if it comes to that. And I hate this place!"

Canyon sighed. "Looks like you've got me over a barrel."

She brightened—then smiled devilishly. "Hey, mister. You take me with you and I'll have you over something else."

"That a promise?"

"I promise," she said eagerly.

"How'd you get in here?"

"The deputy Colson is asleep on his cot inside the office."

"You just walked in past him?"

Her eyes glinted malevolently. "Don' worry. He's out cold. Dead drunk."

"How'd you manage that?"

"I brought him a bottle and then I pleasured him while he drank it."

She'd been a very busy little vixen, it seemed. "Go back and get the keys to this cell—and bring me my six-gun."

She nodded quickly, turned and ran lightly down the hallway. He saw her carefully press open the door, then vanish into the office. He thought he heard a light scuffle, but a moment later she came hurrying toward him, the key ring in one hand, Canyon's six-gun in the other.

"Did I hear a scuffle," he asked her.

She shrugged. "The big fool. He opened his eyes when I was taking the key ring from his belt."

"What'd you do?"

She shuddered slightly. "I clubbed him with your gun.

"Let me have it while you unlock the cell."

She handed his Colt through the bars to him and then began trying the keys on the ring to find the one that fit the door's lock. Meanwhile, Canyon checked the revolver's load, then stuck the Colt back into his holster. Teresa found the right key and pulled the door open. Canyon left the cell and preceded her down the corridor. She was about to hurry past him into the office when he blocked her progress with his right arm. He had heard some movement inside the office. He peered cautiously around the doorjamb and saw the deputy standing groggily in the center of the office, a double-barreled Greener in his hand. It was leveled at the doorway. Canyon ducked back just as the Greener's barrels belched fire.

The wall beside Canyon shredded as the buck shot tore into it. Terrified, Teresa stifled a cry. Canyon poked his six-gun around the doorjamb and pumped three quick shots into the room. Amid the thunderous reverberations, he heard the Greener thump to the floor, followed by the sound of a man's body dropping beside it. Cautiously, Canyon peered into the room. Colson was sprawled facedown on the floor, partially covering the shotgun, a widening rivulet of blood seeping out from under his body.

"Listen!" Teresa cried, hurrying to the window.

Canyon heard the cries also and peered over her shoulder through the window. With Marshal Brothers in the lead, a gun-toting mob was surging down the street, flaring torches casting a lurid glow over the sea of grim faces. Colson's shotgun blast and his own three shots had thoroughly alerted the men that had been gathering for the lynching. They knew trouble was afoot and, from the looks of them, they were anxious not to let Canyon escape their rope.

"Oh, my God!" Teresa cried as the mob filled the street in front of the jail. "We're too late!"

"Maybe not," Canyon told her as he slid a beam in place across the door.

He took Teresa's arm and, hurrying from the

office, he pulled her down the hallway after him to the window. Lifting the sash, he boosted her out into the back alley.

"Get my palomino and gear from the stable— and a mount for yourself. I'll meet you in the alley at the north end of town."

"What are you going to do?"

"Stall them. Hurry! Don't let them see you!"

She was gone on the instant, swallowed up in the darkness. Canyon hurried back into the office as heavy boots trampled up onto the low porch. Someone tried to enter. Finding the door barred, the men on the porch cried out and a moment later came the thump as one or two of them hurled themselves at the door. It was a flimsy door and Canyon saw the beam bending slightly under the assault. The shouts of others back in the crowd urging them on came clearly through the door and Canyon realized that before long a battering ram would be brought up to smash through the door.

Canyon swung the barrel of his six-gun through the lamp on the town marshal's desk. The kerosene splattered across the floor, the base of the lamp following after it, disgorging more liquid. Canyon lifted the lamp's base off the floor and emptied the remainder of the kerosene over a wider area. He took down another lamp hanging from a nail and smashed it against the wall, struck a match and tossed it onto the floor. With a dull *whump* the kerosene caught. The flames raced across the floor, swept over Colson's body—then up the far wall. In a moment they were licking greedily at the ceiling.

There were more shouts from outside the jail

and then fists pounding on the door. Canyon fired two quick shots through it. From the other side came startled cries of pain and surprise. He sent a third round through one of the windows, shattering it. Another sharp outcry was followed by the sound of heavy feet pounding frantically off the porch. With his forearm held up to his face to protect himself from the roaring flames, Canyon backed out of the office and into the cell block hallway. A townsman's head and shoulders were poking through the window at its far end, a revolver gleaming in his hand.

As Canyon raced toward him, the townsman raised his revolver and fired. The shot went wild. Canyon kept on and smashed the gun out of the man's hand before he could fire again, then lowered his shoulders and bowled through the window, driving the man back out into the alley, a shower of glass and window sash coming out with them. Canyon landed on top of the townsman, who offered no resistance as Canyon pushed himself erect. The townsman had been knocked cold. Canyon turned and ran down the alley, the lynch crowd swarming into the alley after him, their quaking torches sending a fitful light ahead of Canyon.

He saw a doorway that led into the rear of a building. Ducking through it, he found himself in a restaurant's small kitchen. Past the astonished cook he darted, then out the door and across the street into an alley. Keeping in its shadows, he raced along. Behind him he heard growing cries for the formation of a bucket brigade and, glancing back, saw a growing crowd surging about the flaming jail. With grim satisfaction he noted how brilliant the night sky over Silver Creek had become.

He had not lost his pursuers, however. Two men hung doggedly on his tail, every now and then sending wild shots after him. When one slug came uncomfortably close, Canyon decided to end this nonsense. He ducked into a dark doorway and waited. Puffing hard, the two pounded past. Canyon stepped out of the doorway, overtook one of them, and brought him down with a blow from his Colt. The fellow's hat went flying, and he cried out as he stumbled forward to the ground. His companion spun around, bringing up his revolver. Canyon ducked back into the shadows as the man fired, the flash from his muzzle lancing through the night. Aiming at the muzzle flash, Canyon fired back—and heard the round punch into the man's flesh. Gasping in surprise, the fellow crumpled to the ground.

Canyon swept past the two men and continued on down the alley. Leaving it a few moments later, he was racing out of town, wondering where in the hell Teresa was, when he heard the thunder of hooves behind him. He turned. Teresa, astride a huge black, was bearing down on him, leading his palomino. She rode astride like a man, her long skirts pulled up to her waist, her underpants visible where she forked the saddle. Slowing as she overtook him, she flung the palomino's reins at him.

He grabbed them and swung into his saddle, clapped his heels to the palomino, and followed after her. As they left the town behind, clattering past a ghostly clump of cottonwood, Canyon looked back. Silver Creek was in turmoil. A confused, milling crowd was still trying to contain the flames—which by now had spread to the buildings adjacent to the jail. From out of the roiling black smoke, the flames winked at Canyon like devils' eyes.

And there was not a single rider in pursuit.

They made a dry camp high on a ridge, one that gave Canyon an excellent view of the bright, moonlit trail below—and of any pursuers that might still be after them. As he finished unrolling his soogan, Teresa moved close to him. He straightened up and turned to her.

"I know where Lance Caulder is," she said.

"Where?"

"An abandoned mining town. There's a saloon and a few buildings left. It's where he will deliver his herd to the buyer from Utah. And Karl Berkick's with him.

"How do you know this?"

"The hostler told me. He overheard Brothers and Lance talking while he was saddling Lance and Berdick's mounts."

"How come he told you?"

"Pete likes me."

"Enough to let you take my horse and give you that big black?"

"You find that hard to believe?"

"Depends on how old he is. When I left my horse in the livery, he looked pretty far gone to me."

She laughed softly. "Pete's old, but not dead

114

yet. It's been a long time since he closed his lips around the nipple on a white breast."

He grinned at her. "Is that what kept you?"

"Pete took out his store teeth and I unbuttoned my bodice. I never wear a corset." She smiled wickedly. "I didn't begrudge him. It did wonders for his morale."

"I can imagine. How far is this abandoned town?"

"Half a day's ride," she replied, moving closer, "maybe a little more."

"Then we better get some shut-eye."

"Yes," she said.

"You . . . don't have a sleeping blanket?" he asked.

"All I have is what I am wearing now. I have given up everything for you, Mr. O'Grady."

"Call me Canyon."

She was pressed hard against him now and, despite his need for sleep, he found himself responding. She was not entirely accurate, of course. What she had given up for him was only what she was desperately eager to abandon, a town she herself described as a hell hole. But she *had* saved his life. He owed her.

And maybe he owed himself, too.

He pulled her closer. She went up on tiptoes and lifted her face to his. He kissed her on the lips and found them hot, pulsing, opening eagerly to the pressure of his lips. In a moment they had both stripped and were scrambling in under the flaps of his soogan.

"Mmm," she murmured, wrapping her long limbs about his thighs. "When I gave old Pete my tit back there, I must admit, it started something for me."

Canyon chuckled. "You mean you got an itch you want me to scratch."

"Yes," she said. "Now shut up and get on with it."

His big hand dropped to her moist pubis. She sighed and opened her thighs. He plastered his lips onto hers. Clinging to him, she swung her body under his. He nudged her thighs wider with his knee. Already her moist pubis had touched the tip of his erection.

"I can feel you! Go in! What are you waiting for?"

He chuckled and nudged in past her labia. Her fingers flew down his flanks, and with a swift, heated urgency that aroused him even more, she grasped his buttocks and flung her body up at him and sucked him still deeper into her. Raw with desire, he thrust full and deep, grunting with the exertion. She moaned from deep within her and fastened her lips to his, her tongue probing wildly as she brought her legs up and locked her ankles around his back. With each thrust she hugged him still tighter, her hips grinding as she sucked him still deeper into her.

Pulling back, careful not to withdraw entirely, he then thrust back in, deeper, this time hitting bottom. He felt Teresa shudder under the impact. She opened her mouth to gasp, her head thrown back, her eyes shut tightly as he continued his long, deep plunges, driving fiercely into her until he felt himself moving inexorably toward his own climax. Tiny, inarticulate cries broke from Teresa's throat. She began twisting her head from side to side. Still deeper he thrust, rocking her violently, slamming into her with such intensity it felt as if a switch had been turned on deep in his groin.

Teresa cried out, a high, piercing shriek, and he felt her go rigid under him. Her vaginal muscles tightened convulsively. With a sudden powerful thrust, he nailed her to the ground and both of them came then in a long, shuddering orgasm that left Canyon limp, still deep within her moist, clasping pocket, coming again and again in a series of uncontrollable spasms that only gradually subsided.

A blissful relief engulfed him. He fell forward onto her, his shaft still enclosed in her soft, warm snugness, her legs still scissored about his waist. She did not want to let him go, it seemed.

"You came near death this night," she whispered. "So now you feel life surging through you— and I feel it too, flowing into me. It was wonderful, Canyon."

"I didn't mind it, either."

"Then don't you dare roll off me now and go to sleep. I am just coming awake to a real man. It does not happen often to a girl in my profession."

He chuckled softly, his face buried in the luxuriant abundance of her fragrant hair. "I hear you."

"Good!"

Teresa rolled over onto him, still holding him with her legs. A moment later she was fully astride him, her head thrown back, the lines of her neck muscles taut. She began to rock slowly back and forth, allowing the lips of her vagina to caress his erection. At first it had little effect, but she was patient. Gradually, with maddening deliberation, she increased her pace. Canyon felt the first faint ache growing within his loins. It was not long before he felt himself growing larger, surging upward into her. Moaning, Teresa increased her tempo, driving deeper now with each thrust, impaling herself eagerly on Canyon's erection with fierce, reckless abandon.

He reached up and cupped her breasts in his big, rough hands. She nodded her head frantically.

"Yes!" she cried fiercely. "I want that! Yes!"

Canyon felt her erect nipples, hard as bullets, thrusting against his palms. Her movements became more violent. No longer was she thrusting up and down. Now she was moving back and forth along the length of his erection, turning it to fire. He cried out as sudden urgency flared in his loins. She grinned down at him, blowing a wet lock of hair off her face. He dropped his hands from her breasts and grabbed her hips to increase the pace of her horizontal thrusting—nearing his climax now, frantic she not pull all the way out.

"Faster!" she cried, her voice hoarse with need. "Faster! And deeper! Deeper, damn you! I want all of you!"

He did his best to oblige and she flung herself forward onto him, her thick veil of hair falling over him, her lips fastening to his. He opened his mouth and her tongue darted frantically in, flicking like a snake's. In an agony of desire, he flung up his buttocks so violently that he nearly catapulted her over his shoulders. She cried out in the pure wild joy of it, and he let go of her hips and encircled her shoulders, still holding his mouth hard against hers, their tongues entwined, her hips grinding down on him now with a control that was as amazing as it was effective, welding them in a passionate dance that had become sheer instinct. Abruptly Canyon felt himself exploding deep within her. She flung her head back and cried out as she too climaxed, her inner muscles opening and contracting, sucking his erection clean. Clinging to each other, shuddering, the storm gradually subsided—until at last Teresa collapsed onto his chest, gasping with delight.

In the moonlight her face gleamed with perspiration. Panting softly, she raised her face to look full into his eyes, then covered his face with soft, playful kisses. She was in a transport of delight, pleasing Canyon as much as it pleased her. When she slid off him finally, it was slowly, lingeringly.

"That was so nice," she told him softly, brushing his damp locks off his forehead.

"You did seem to enjoy it."

"When you are lying on your back allowing dirty men to plow you with drunken abandon—when all you do is haul their ashes—believe me, Canyon, you lose some of your enthusiasm."

"I can imagine that."

"Of course, maybe that is good. You no longer care and do not want to care. Caring for such men would be fatal. But every once in a while such a woman as me wonders what it would be like to find a man such as you."

"Well, you really let loose this time, all right."

"Ah, it was so good. The way it used to be when I was young and wicked and took the young boys behind the barn. I wonder now if I could ever go back to that sad profession. It's a good living, I suppose—if you put something by for a rainy day—but I tell you, Canyon, something in me was beginning to die."

"That's why you wanted out of Silver Creek."

"Yes. And out of that life. Thank you, Canyon, for helping me."

"I should be thanking you. I'd be dancing from a noose right now if you hadn't come for me."

"Then you won't abandon me? I have only the clothes on my back—and this horse."

"That's a fine piece of horseflesh, and those duds should last until we get you to Placer City."

She kissed him again, then moved her long, silken limbs close against his under the soogan's blanket. He closed his eyes. Sleep turned his limbs to heavy logs. He closed his eyes and felt himself drifting.

Teresa's hand closed about his and a moment later he was asleep.

They reached the abandoned mining town late the next day. Huddled in a narrow canyon below the mine entrance were a few ramshackle buildings split by a narrow road. He saw the saloon Teresa had mentioned, the shell of a general store alongside it, and across the road from that, a two-story building with hardly a single window intact. Against the nearby mountainside, he made out the yellow scars of mine dumps and the scaffolding of mine structures stripped of their covering timber. Near the mine entrance, the crumbling skeleton of a stamping mill stood out starkly against the slope.

Leaving Teresa high in the rocks with their

mounts, Canyon reconnoitered the town. Perched on a ledge above the saloon, he caught the dim scuff of movement below him and the low mutter of voices coming from the building across the road. Lance Caulder passed out of the saloon and crossed to the building, disappearing behind it. Four dusty horses stood patiently at the hitch-rail in front of the saloon. Behind the saloon there was a horse barn and from it Canyon could hear the occasional stamping of horses, and from the saloon's back yard every now and then came the cluck of foraging chickens.

Canyon hunkered down to wait.

In about ten minutes two men strode from the saloon, mounted up, and rode out. As they rode past him on their way out of town, he got a much better glimpse of their scarred, ferretlike faces; they were more than likely outlaws on the run, this town serving as an ideal place to hole up.

Two horses remained at the hitch-rail. Canyon waited a little longer, then returned to Teresa.

"Lance is down there. I saw him. I didn't see his foreman. But there's two horses in front of the saloon, so I figure Berdick's down there somewhere with him."

"You're going after them?"

He nodded, checking the load in his Colt. Then he handed Teresa his Henry. "Can you use this?"

She nodded.

"Are you sure?"

"Yes, Canyon. I am sure."

"All right, then. I'll leave it with you to protect yourself if this goes bad."

"Thank you."

He looked at her and saw the light in her eyes and realized how much she was enjoying this. "I won't be long," he told her. "I want to get this over with before dark."

"Are you going to arrest both men?"

"I don't have a warrant."

"Is it true what they say? That you are from Washington and that you have come here to bring Lance Caulder to justice for what he did in the war."

"True enough."

He left her then, working his way back down the slope until he was behind the saloon. The saloon keeper ducked out of the saloon to empty a slops jar, then disappeared back inside. Canyon could hear the sound of pans clattering in the saloon's kitchen.

He moved closer to the chicken house and the hens squawked and fluttered in outrage at his sudden appearance. Sidestepping a fat Rhode Island red, he moved across the yard, mounted the back porch steps, and strode into the saloon's kitchen, his Colt out. A squat, flat-faced Navajo woman looked up from a wood stove. He nodded curtly to her and kept on walking through the small kitchen and came out into the saloon. The owner of the saloon was reaching for a shotgun under the bar as Canyon stepped into the room. Canyon waggled his Colt at him and shook his head. The owner released the shotgun and stepped back. He was a large, balding round-faced fellow with a black patch over one eye.

"No need for that shotgun," Canyon told him.

"Stay out of this and you'll live to eat your supper."

"Who the hell are you?"

"Never mind that," Canyon said, glancing quickly about—unhappy at not finding Karl Berdick in the place.

The owner of the saloon shrugged.

"Where's Berdick and Lance Caulder?"

"This is your party, mister."

"Those two mounts outside. They must belong to somebody."

"Can't argue with that."

"What's your name?"

"My friends call me Wally. It would be Smith to you."

"All right, Smith. Get out from behind the bar."

Smith did as Canyon told him. Canyon reached in under the bar for the shotgun. He broke it open and dumped out the cartridges, then tossed the shotgun to the floor and stepped out the saloon door, heading for the building across the street, the one behind which Lance Caulder had disappeared. He was halfway across the road when he heard a mean chuckle coming from the saloon. Turning, he saw Karl Berdick step into view, his six-gun out and leveled on Canyon's chest.

"You lookin' for someone, deputy?" he snarled, yellow teeth flashing against his unshaven face.

"That's right, Berdick. You and Lance."

Berdick cocked his gun and sighted along the barrel. "I don't know how you got out of Silver Creek, you son of a bitch, but you ain't got a chance in hell of gettin' out of this."

Canyon was about to throw himself to one side

when his Henry's sharp crack came from above. Hit from behind, Berdick staggered, then flung himself about and pumped two quick shots at the ledge where Teresa was crouched. She ducked quickly back out of sight. Canyon finished Berdick with a shot to his head. A shot rang out from an upstairs window in the building behind him. The ground erupted at his feet and kicked up twice more as Canyon ducked back to the saloon, turned the corner, and flattened himself against the wall.

Peering around the corner of the saloon at the second-floor window, Canyon saw what looked like the faint glow of a cigarette tip. Not until it winked out did he realize it was only the sun's last rays glancing off a splinter of glass. As soon as the sun dipped below the surrounding peaks, darkness seeped into the canyon like smoke, obscuring the building. In no hurry at all, Canyon waited for it to grow still darker, confident that Lance could go nowhere, not with his mount still stamping wearily at the hitch-rack in front of the saloon.

At last, as the encroaching darkness gave him the cover he needed, Canyon darted across the road and cut around to the rear of the building. Spotting a door, he pushed it open, stepped inside, and found himself facing a narrow flight of stairs. He cocked his head to listen. The smell of an abandoned place came to him, musty and dry, with the remnant odors of a thousand items once held within it still clinging to the walls and flooring. The tiny, scurrying feet of a rat crossed a hidden beam above him. That was the only sound. Nothing came from the building, from the road on the other side of it, or from the saloon.

But he could sense Lance Caulder crouched in the darkness on the floor above.

He set one foot forward and down, testing the flooring in front of the stairwell, letting his weight fall easy and slow—and found there was no flooring, only solid, hard-packed ground. He kept going until his foot struck the first step. He eased himself up onto it and, testing each board, mounted the stairs until he reached the second-floor landing. A doorway's rectangular opening yawned before him. He was moving cautiously along the landing when the toe of his right boot struck the door sill. Crouching quickly, he waited for the sound to fade, but small as the echo was it seemed to swell ominously into the room beyond. He listened intently, but heard nothing. Even so, he thought he could feel the waiting man crouched in the darkness. He kept himself perfectly still and waited.

A voice, hoarse now and no longer carrying the surly arrogance Canyon remembered, came out of the impenetrable gloom beyond the doorway.

"That you, O'Grady?"

"It's me, all right. Throw down your gun and come out of there."

"You killed Karl."

"He's dead enough, all right."

"I saw the whole thing. You got that hot bitch on your side!"

"Looks like it."

"You think the two of you can take me in?"

"We sure as hell can try."

"This is crazy, O'Grady. Go back to Washington! The war's over!"

"There's still some things that have to be cleaned up."

"I was just following Quantrill's orders."

"You did it with too much enthusiasm, Caulder. And we've got witnesses from those towns you burned after you left Quantrill, and those civilians you strung up and mutilated. The war won't be over for them until you're brought to trial."

"Damn you! You know what'll happen to me at a trial in a Yankee courtroom!"

Lance's voice echoed hollowly in the empty room so that it was impossible for Canyon to tell where he was. The darkness outside was complete by this time and no light at all filtered in through the shattered windows. Edging himself through the doorway, Canyon held his Colt out in front of him, his eyes straining to pick out Caulder in the nearly impenetrable darkness.

A shot lanced out of the darkness, the round smashing into the floor at Canyon's feet. A second shot came after it, this one searing past Canyon's cheek. Throwing himself flat, Canyon aimed at the source of the gunflashes and fired, the streak of light from his own gun barrel blooming blue-crimson in the blackness. Abruptly, from the stairwell behind Canyon came the boom of a shotgun. Buckshot whispered past his left shoulder. He rolled over and kept rolling as the shotgun boomed again, the buckshot chewing up the flooring behind him.

"Come on, Lance!" cried Smith.

Canyon heard Lance jump up, dart past him in the darkness, and hit the stairs at a run. The sound of both men's boots pounding down the stairs filled the room. Canyon got to his feet and rushed to the window. Out from behind the building Lance and the saloon owner galloped. Canyon tracked Lance, fired, and missed. He cocked and fired again. This time, Smith cried out and flipped backward off his horse.

Lance galloped on out of the canyon without a single glance back.

Canyon dropped quickly beside Teresa. "My God, woman," he said. "Why didn't you cry out. I didn't know you were hit."

Flat on her back, her voice came to him faintly. "I didn't want to distract you."

"How bad is it?" Canyon asked foolishly.

"I am hit pretty bad, I think. I cannot stop the bleeding."

Canyon swiftly peeled back Teresa's bodice. What he saw sickened him. One breast was shattered and the blood was flowing from her chest in a steady stream. That she wasn't dead already was a miracle. He sat back on his haunches, not knowing what to do or say. That one of Berdick's wild shots could have found Teresa was appalling.

"Just lie still," he told her. "I've got to stop that bleeding."

"Too late, I think."

"Don't talk like that."

"How did you like that shot of mine?"

"You saved my ass, Teresa."

"It is such a beautiful ass, I am glad. Did you get Lance?"

"He got away."

She sighed. "I will not go to Placer City with you, I am afraid."

"Don't talk nonsense," he scolded her gently. "Once we stop this bleeding, you'll be all right."

He was busy ripping off the bottom of her skirt, intending to wad it up and staunch the blood flowing from her wound, when she stirred fitfully and held out one arm to him.

"Hold me," she whispered. "Now!"

"I want to stop your bleeding."

"Please! My life has been so wicked! Hold me! I am afraid!"

He caught the searing urgency in her voice and quickly pulled her to him. The moment his arms folded about her, there was a soft, almost imperceptible shudder; and when he pulled back to look into her eyes, he saw that the light in them had gone out.

Teresa was right. She was not going to Placer City with him after all.

8

Midafternoon of the next day, back in the high country on Lance Caulder's trail, Canyon came to a small glen that was little more than a wrinkle in the rough, tangled pile of peaks he was traveling through. On its far side, the glen was bounded by a pile of titanic boulders squatting at the base of a towering butte. He stayed in the timber until he reached the butte; then, skirting one of the boulders, he rode out onto the glen and came in sight of a stream, a campfire flickering on its bank.

He pulled up at once and looked about him and saw no one. That didn't mean a thing. Somewhere on the fringe of this clearing a man stood and held a gun leveled on him. Canyon knew that because of the frying pan beside the fire and the blackened pot with the hot coffee steaming in it. He dismounted slowly and stood quietly in front of the palomino, feeling his danger.

"All right," he announced quietly, lifting his head slightly as he looked around. "Whoever you are, no need to come out shooting."

He heard a scrape behind him, then the chink of spurs as a boot came down on a solid stretch of cap rock. Without a word, a man walked past him with a revolver in his hand. He dropped it into his flapped, black leather Navy holster, paused by his fire and turned to look at Canyon. He was a man in his early forties with a tough, leathery face, thin now with a weariness that seemed bone-deep. He pointed to the fire.

"Just finished my noon camp. All I got left is some jerky and coffee. You're welcome to it."

"Thanks," Canyon said, turning back to the palomino. "I'd appreciate that."

Canyon offsaddled his horse, dumped the saddle against the base of a tree, then set the animal loose to crop the fresh green sward at the edge of the clearing. By this time, the man had placed a frying pan on the flames and was sitting on a log watching the jerky in it sizzle.

"Name's O'Grady," Canyon told the older man as he approached the fire. "Canyon O'Grady."

"Jack Tenny. I owned the Hatchet, still do, what's left of it."

"You're the one Lance Caulder burnt out."

"He burnt me out and took my cattle. The son of a bitch. How come you know all this?"

"Sam Gills."

"Then you're the one."

"What do you mean?"

"The one who's after Caulder, stirrin' up this mess."

"You think I'm the one responsible, do you?"

Tenny filled a cup with coffee and handed it to Canyon. "Hell, no. All that bastard wanted was an excuse to move against us, and I guess you provided it. I don't blame him, though." Tenny chuckled. "We been cuttin' down the bastard's herds some, and that's a fact."

"You don't deny it?"

"Why should I? Them gray coats are johnny-come-latelys to this country, and now they want it all to themselves. We had to fight the Navajos, the Apaches, and the Utes—and then they come in to reap what we sowed. Sure, me and Gills been whittlin' at their herds."

"And now they're moving on you."

"Yep."

"Well, you and Sam got help coming. Jim Swallows of the Big J is throwing in with you."

"What's that you say?"

"I mean he's on his way up here now to join Sam Gills. Probably already at the Lazy S by now."

"How come Jim Swallows is throwin' in with us poor white trash ranchers."

"Caulder burnt out the Sun Ranch and wounded Steadman pretty bad."

Tenny pursed his lips. "I already heard. Steadman's dead. And Swallows is sweet on Helen Steadman. I guess a blind man could see the connection."

Canyon frowned at the thought of Steadman's death, but he could not say he was surprised. "How far is the Lazy S?"

Tenny grinned at him. "You havin' trouble findin' your way around this here rough country?"

"You might say that."

"The Lazy S is over that ridge behind me. 'Pears to me you were headin' in the right direction."

Canyon sat down on the log beside Tenny. By this time the jerky was sizzling in the frying pan;

Canyon gulped some of the steaming coffee and watched as Tenny dumped some of the jerky onto a tin plate. Tenny handed the plate to him. Canyon took it, pulled out his pocket knife and began eating the meat. Eating alongside him, Tenny glanced behind Canyon at the grazing palomino.

"Your palomino looks plumb tuckered out. Man shouldn't drive a mount into the ground like that."

"I had no choice," Canyon told him, using the last of his coffee to wash down the jerky.

"You got fellers on your tail?"

"No. I'm trying to catch up to Lance Caulder."

"What're you aimin' to do when you get the man."

"Haul him out of here—take him back to Washington. There's a rope waiting for him."

"Eat up then, and welcome."

Canyon finished the jerky and poured himself another cup of coffee, then glanced sidelong at Tenny.

"What are you doing here, Tenny?"

"Waiting for my riders to show. We're going after that herd of mine Caulder took. One of my men found out where his men stashed it."

"Where might that be?"

"A hidden valley not far from here."

"How long before your riders arrive? I might want to join you and your men. See what develops. Lance wouldn't be very far from that herd, I'm thinking. He's already found a buyer for it in Silver Creek."

Tenny cocked an eyebrow and rubbed his stubbled jaw reflectively. It sounded like a file on sandpaper. Then he lifted the pan off the fire and slapped it a couple of times with the side of his tin cup. A man stepped out of the brush across the clearing. Canyon heard movement to his right and, glancing in that direction, saw two men step into view from behind a boulder. Four more left the timber fringing the clearing and at a nod from Tenny, the men started walking toward them. Every man jack of them carried a rifle.

"Here's my men," Tenny said. "And they're worth twenty of Lance Caulder's gray coats."

"I count only seven," Canyon replied. "You really think that's enough to stop Lance Caulder?"

"I don't need an army. All I want is a clear shot at that son of a bitch. So maybe we don't need Swallows."

"How far is this valley?"

"Not far. Follow me."

Tenny stood up and headed for the butte, his men trailing behind him. At the edge of the glen, they reached a narrow game trail that wound up the side of the butte. The climb was steep, and when they reached the top, Canyon saw two more of Tenny's men with binoculars crouched behind two fat boulders on the rim. Leaving Canyon, Tenny walked over to confer with his two lookouts. Looking out over the mountains from this height, Canyon saw great, anvil-topped thunderheads building over the peaks. Lightning winked and flickered deep in their black bowels. There was an oppressive, muggy closeness in the air, and Canyon realized that a thunderstorm was a certainty before this day was out.

He walked to the edge of the butte and peered down into the long, winding valley where he pre-

sumed Tenny and his men were sure Lance Caulder
had driven the stolen cattle. He peered closely at
the forested slopes and the few open meadows. If
the herd was down in that valley somewhere, it
was pretty well hidden. Not a single head was
visible.

Tenny approached him.

"Lance Caulder rode up not long ago and disappeared into that valley." He looked closely at Canyon. "My men said he was really smokin' that
horse of his. Guess you lit a fire under him."

"I tried to do a lot worse."

"Tell you what, O'Grady. I say we don't wait for
Gills or Swallows. I say we go in right now—while
it's still daylight."

Canyon glanced again at the sky. The storm
clouds had not yet blotted out the sun, and por-
tions of the sky were still a bright blue; but the
clouds were building fast. If they were going to go
in after Caulder, they had better make their move
soon. The important thing for Canyon to remember was that Lance was in that valley—and it was
Lance he was after, not Tenny's rustled cattle.

"Okay," he said to Tenny. "Let's go."

Canyon and Tenny—his Hatchet riders close
behind them—broke out into a marshy area. The
trail ahead of them now became pocked with hoof
marks, and Canyon saw places where it was obvious some of the rustled cattle had become bogged.
He could see clearly the tracks left by struggling
horses and in more than a few places saw where
men's boots had been sucked deep into the marshy
ground as the men struggled to free the cattle.

They kept on, topped a ridge, and followed the trail down through a heavy patch of timber. Breaking from it, they came upon the herd grazing in a broad parkland. Immediately, they turned their horses and rode back into the cover of the timber. The clouds Canyon had observed earlier were now directly overhead. Dim peals of thunder had been grumbling in the distance, while forks of lightning winked about the valley's encircling peaks. It was only a matter of time before the clouds over their heads opened up.

Canyon saw through the trees the backs of at least four hundred head of cattle. The herd was quiet. It looked as if had already bedded down for the night. Astride his horse, Canyon shucked his hat back off his forehead and shook his head in amazement. Not until that moment had it dawned on him just how massive a bite Lance Caulder was taking out of the hill ranchers' cattle.

Tenny and Canyon dismounted and, with Tenny in the lead, they all led their horses around the rim of the herd, heading for a campfire all of them could see pulsing dimly on the far side. They had made their way more than a hundred yards closer to the campfire when Canyon pulled up abruptly. He could discern no movement around the fire and realized that it was a decoy. He turned to Tenny.

"Forget that campfire. There's no one around it."

Tenny nodded quickly. He had already come to the same conclusion. Crowding around Tenny and Canyon, the Hatchet riders began looking nervously about them.

"Hey!" someone muttered, pointing. "Look! Over there!"

Riders were pushing through the herd directly toward them, and behind them other riders were racing along the fringe of the herd, intent on cutting them off.

"Damn it," Tenny muttered. "We walked right into this one. We better get back into the timber."

"Think again," counseled Canyon. "If we turn our backs on them now, they'll just cut us down at their leisure, like shooting fish in a rain barrel. I say we mount up and stampede that herd back at them, then keep the herd going until we're out of this."

Tenny nodded grimly. "We'll do it."

Canyon swung up onto the palomino and unholstered his Colt. Tenny mounted up also and raised his six-gun and punched a hole in the night sky. A ragged chorus of gunfire from the Hatchet riders joined his and as the thunderous detonations rolled across the herd, the cattle leaped to their feet as one single animal and stampeded away from the gunfire. Keeping after the herd, Canyon punched his own shots into the air over the plunging sea of backs as Tenny's men spread out in a long line on both sides of him.

In full flight now, the herd plunged through the growing darkness in a reasonably straight course, the soul-chilling thunder of their pounding hooves filling the air. Ahead of him, Canyon caught the flash of gunfire as Caulder's men tried to turn or split the herd. Their efforts were futile; but they managed to crowd the herd's leaders and Canyon heard the sound of clicking horns as the cattle came together. Some of the cattle, crazed with fear, milled frantically, a few just behind the leaders rearing up and riding over them—the broiling mass squirming like a nest of bristling snakes.

By this time most of Caulder's riders were caught up in the plunging torrent. Some of them were trying to outrun the cattle. Others, overtaken or caught in the cattle's midst, struggled to keep in their saddles, shooting wildly about them in a desperate effort to force a way out of this headlong stream. Some did not make it as horse and rider were caught up in the relentless tide and trampled under.

It was fully dark by now and Canyon felt his horse plunge over the lip of a steep gully. The palomino lit heavily, stumbled forward and went to its knees. Canyon hauled it back up onto its feet and booted the horse up the far bank of the gully. Once more in sight of the herd, Canyon saw that it had narrowed into a massive stream funneling between the timbered slopes leading out of the valley. And Tenny's men were visible now in full pursuit of those of Caulder's riders who had managed to survive the stampede. Hot lead filled the air as the two forces flung shots at each other. Men cried out and horses whinnied in terror as they were struck by bullets or dragged to the ground by wounded riders. Gunflashes lit the night eerily.

Abruptly—as if anxious to join the fray—the cloudburst that had been gathering all afternoon burst full upon them with an unnerving, shattering impact. Thunder rent the air with a palpable force that almost drove Canyon off his horse. Lightning flickered and flashed almost constantly, playing a hideous blue light over the plunging backs of the stampeding cattle. Then came the incredible, lashing downpour, a mean, stinging assault on him and his palomino. He kept on nevertheless, following after the stampeding cattle, who now plunged on in renewed terror. Before long, Canyon passed the marshy spot they had come upon when entering the valley. The marshy spot now was deep in swirling water and should have slowed the cattle some; but they did not hesitate as they charged on blindly through the exploding night.

Canyon was not entirely aware when it was he realized they had managed to put the valley behind them. At any rate, the going—for him and the cattle, at least—was considerably easier as they continued on across a high, treeless plateau. Ahead of him through the slanting curtains of rain, he made out a few of Tenny's riders keeping pace with the surging cattle.

Then he saw Tenny. The owner of the Hatchet was going after one of Caulder's riders, sending continuous fire after the fleeing horseman. Digging his heels into the palomino's flanks, Canyon urged it after Tenny. As he was about to overtake Tenny, he caught sight of another Caulder rider coming at Tenny from the man's blind side. To head him off, Canyon cut toward him.

But the sudden change in direction was too much for the nearly spent palomino. The animal lost its footing on the mud-slicked ground and went down instantly, flinging Canyon over its neck. He somersaulted in midair, his back striking the ground with numbing force. He was still holding his Colt, but felt his grip slacken, and the Colt went flying as he slid wildly over the slick ground. A man-sized boulder embedded in the ground reared up before him and slammed him on the side of his head.

Lights exploded deep in his skull and he spun off into darkness.

When Canyon regained consciousness, the rain was still coming down. He felt as if every bone in his body had been fractured. He rolled over and was about to sit up when he saw two horsemen—Lance Caulder and Jim Swallows—riding through the rain toward him. Before they reached the boulder, they pulled to a halt, their shoulders hunched against the driving rain.

"Ah could use some of your riders," Caulder told Swallows, his voice coming clearly through the downpour. "Three of my men are dead and the rest've lit out for God knows where."

"There's no chance of that, Lance. It's best for both of us this way. I've already talked Gills into holding off any action for now."

"But hell, Jim, you know ah can't stand still for this!"

"Maybe you better lay low until this blows over. Tenny's not going to be an easy man to stop. And I can't keep Gills quiet much longer. And then there's that wild card—O'Grady."

"That's one pure son of a bitch. But he ain't stoppin' me and I ain't layin' low. Ah'm goin' to keep the pressure on these hill ranchers until they give way."

Swallows shrugged. "Just so I get my share."

"You'll have the Sun Ranch—and Helen. What more d'you all want?"

"Okay, okay," Swallows told him. "Do it your way."

Jim Swallows, it seemed, was no match for Lance Caulder—and apparently never had been. That show he had put on when he turned back Lance had been just that. A show. One he had put on for his men. It would not do for them—or Helen—to know he had thrown in with Lance Caulder.

The two men started up again and loomed closer. Canyon could see them through his slitted eyelids. For a moment he thought they would ride on past without seeing him. But then they both pulled up.

"Hey!" Caulder said, leaning over to peer down at Canyon's sprawled body. "Is that who I think it is?"

"Jesus! You're right! It's O'Grady!"

"Ah knew that son of a bitch had something to do with this."

"Your luck's changing, Lance. Looks like O'Grady bought it."

"Maybe so, but ah better make sure."

Caulder nudged his horse closer, dismounted, and kicked Canyon viciously in his side. Canyon suffered the blow without wincing and kept his eyes closed, his face slack. Caulder kicked him a second time, then leaned closer to study Canyon's face.

"He hit that boulder, smashed his head," Caulder said.

"Yeah, I can see the blood."

Caulder straightened and stepped back. "Go ahead, Swallows. Finish him off."

"Why me?"

"Ah just want to see if you've got the sand for it."

"You know I can't do that, Lance. This man has shared a jug with me on my porch."

"You sound like an old woman."

"You're the one he's after. You finish him."

With a shrug, Caulder took out his revolver, stepped back, and cocked it. Peering up at Lance from under his eyelids, Canyon caught the wet gun barrel's dull glint. Before he could fling himself aside, Caulder fired. Flame leaped from the muzzle. The bullet glanced off the side of his skull, a fearsome blow that slammed his head to one side. He seemed to lift off the ground and twist slowly, weightlessly into darkness. But he did not pass out entirely as the grating sound of Caulder's laughter dragged him back to consciousness. He felt Caulder's rough hands drag him out of the mud and fling him over his saddle's pommel. Caulder swung up onto the saddle behind him, and for an interminable time, they rode on through the downpour.

Abruptly, Caulder's horse turned and Canyon felt himself being flung out into space. He came to earth hard, his body crashing through brush and slamming over low boulders sleek with rain. He cartwheeled through bracken and brush alders until he plunged facedown into a raging torrent sweeping through a ravine and was caught up immediately in its brutal flow. He turned twice, sank below the surface, then slammed finally up against a sand bank. He pushed his shoulders and head out of the water and grabbed hold of a boulder to keep himself from being swept on farther.

Above the continuing pound of the rain, he heard approaching hoofbeats and then the dim murmur of conversation high above him. Without moving his head, he managed to see Caulder and Swallows sitting their horses at the edge of the ravine as they peered down at him. Evidently deciding a few parting shots would not hurt any, they drew their sidearms and opened up on him, laughing like youngsters in a dump shooting at bottles and tin cans.

As the hot slugs seared into the water about Canyon's shoulders, he let the silt-laden water pluck him off the sand bar and carry him farther downstream until, well out of sight of Swallows and Caulder, he struck against the side of a large boulder and hung on. Only when he heard the fading mutter of Caulder's and Swallows's hoofbeats did he release his hold on the boulder and drag himself out onto a steep, rocky slope. There he collapsed as the pounding rain massaged him into a sweet oblivion.

It was daylight when he awoke, with just enough light to show him the steep sides of the gully. The rain had slackened some, but his teeth were chattering wildly. He felt the furrow in his scalp left by Caulder's bullet and found it was not serious. His thick head, it seemed, was a match for any bullet. He clawed his way out of the gully and got to his feet. Despite that plunge into the arroyo, nothing was broken, just a few bolts and hinges loosened some.

He started walking, his eyes peering intently at the ground, looking for signs. Soon enough he came upon the trail left by the stampeding cattle, but the rain had washed out most of their tracks. He kept walking, saw a horse on its side thrashing feebly. He would have shot the poor brute, but his Colt was somewhere back along the trail.

A few minutes later, he pulled up. Less than twenty yards from him, his palomino was standing in the light drizzle, its head drooping forlornly. Canyon called softly to it. The horse's ears flickered hopefully at sight of him and nickered softly. Canyon moved cautiously toward him and called out a second time. That did it. Though the palomino watched him warily, it allowed Canyon to move close enough to grab its reins and pull it closer. Fitting his boot into the stirrup, Canyon hauled his right leg over the cantle and straightened up in the saddle. He patted the palomino's neck gently, then pulled it around and rode back the way he had come, his eyes searching the ground, hoping against hope he would find his Colt.

And then he saw the gleam of his six-gun's cylinder and barrel, its ivory handle almost entirely buried in the mud. And, sitting on the ground beside it was his hat, resting crown up. He dismounted, picked up the weapon and examined it. It would need to be cleaned entirely, but at least he still had it. He dropped it into his holster and plucked his hat off the ground. He cleaned off the sweat band with his forefinger, then put it on, doing his best to ignore the sharp stab of pain that came from the gash in his skull.

He hauled his creaking limbs back into his saddle, wondering what time it was. He glanced up through the light rain and thought he could see the sun's placement through the thinning clouds. It was almost noon. Plenty of time had elasped since he and Tenny's men had stampeded that herd.

And now Canyon had much to think over.

Jim Swallows was playing a lone hand. None of his riders—and certainly not Helen Steadman—was aware of his link with Lance Caulder. Swallows's motivation was clear enough. With the hill ranchers driven out, there would be plenty of land for Swallows and the other big cattlemen. To top it off, Swallows would gain access to the Sun Ranch, the largest hill spread adjacent to his own land.

And Helen Steadman would end up married to the man who, all this time, had been in league with her father's killer.

9

Close on to nightfall, Canyon came upon a homesteader's log cabin high in the range on the edge of a narrow belt of stream-fed meadowland. The soil here, Canyon could not help noting, was thin, the grass precariously rooted. All these factors the homesteader's place accurately reflected.

The cabin was ringed with pinon stumps. Its roof was a mélange of timber and brush. The privy sat crookedly behind the cabin on an uneven hole dug halfheartedly from the stony soil. Littering the front yard was a discouraging assortment of rusted farm implements, a rotting mattress, a buggy missing three wheels, and an overturned grindstone. Only the pole barn seemed to be the result of a solid effort on the homesteader's part.

A few chickens scratching in the front yard scattered at his approach, clucking indignantly. A ragged-looking collie left the barn to bark at him. The combined racket brought the homesteader out onto his low porch. He was carrying a Hawken. A sharp rebuke sent the collie back into the barn. Behind the homesteader came his wife, a large, swollen, lank-haired creature of Navajo ancestry. The rotting porch sagged dangerously under her prodigious weight.

Canyon reined in the palomino and waited for the homesteader to lower his Hawken. When he did, Canyon nodded to his woman.

"Howdy, ma'am,"

She muttered something to her husband. Then she scratched the crack in her ass and vanished back into the house.

"I'm looking for the Dixieland spread," Canyon told the homesteader.

Without replying, the man regarded Canyon sourly, his sunken cheeks and cadaverous frame mute testimony to his lack of success in this region. His examination of Canyon complete, he expectorated a black gob of chewing tobacco at a plant poking up beside his porch.

"You got a ways to go yet, mister. But you're welcome to light and set a spell. There's plenty of water and oats for your hoss. And for supper we got some potatoes and roots, if you've a mind to join us."

Canyon nodded. It was a poor sort of man who turned down any offer of hospitality. "Thanks," he told the homesteader.

"See to your hoss, then. I'll tell my woman to set another place at the table."

He went back inside.

Canyon swung stiffly out of his saddle and led the palomino into the barn. Though the rain had stopped hours before, he had ridden through a gray, sunless world and the dampness had seeped deep into his bones. He hoped there would be a wood fire inside.

But there was no wood fire and the one room interior of the cabin was a fetid cell lit by a single coal oil lamp hung from a rafter. It took an anxious moment or two for Canyon to accustom his stomach to the cabin's awesome stench, one compounded of coal oil, unwashed bodies, and rotting swill.

The roots the homesteader had mentioned turned out to be turnips. Together with the potatoes simmering in a thick, meaty broth, they made for a supper hearty enough to warm Canyon's insides clear down to his boot heels. He made it a point not to ask what kind of meat the woman used in the stew.

The meal finished, the homesteader—his name was Ben Koker—reached under the table for a jug of corn liquor and passed it across to Canyon. He lifted the jug to his mouth. A moment later, as he wiped off his mouth and blinked the tears from his eyes, he wondered if he hadn't just swallowed pure lit kerosene. He handed the jug back to Koker. The man lifted it high, swallowed twice, then handed the jug over to his wife. Flower was her name and she had been waiting eagerly. She snatched the jug and took two long swallows, wiped her lips, then took two more.

Canyon saw the alarm on Koker's face. "Flower, you hold up some," he snapped. "Don't take advantage we got ourselves a guest here."

Reluctantly, Flower handed the jug back to her husband. He took a quick swig, then placed the jug down on the table between him and Canyon.

"You're on your way to Lance Caulder's spread," he said. "That right?"

Canyon nodded.

"What's your business with that gray coat?"

"That's none of your business, Koker."

"He a friend of yours, is he?"

"No."

"Well, he's no friend of mine, neither. All that beef he's got and the son of a bitch resents it when I rescue one or two of his scraggly head to feed my family."

"What's the best trail to the Dixieland?"

Koker shrugged. "Just keep on over the ridge the way you was going. You'll dip into a valley. Go east then over a ridge for at least a couple of hours until you come to a long flat and you'll see the Dixieland buildings."

"How long a ride is it?"

"Half a day's ride, maybe."

"Guess I'll get a move on, then."

Koker reached for the jug and handed it to Canyon. "No need for that. Stay the night. Here, take another swig of this."

Canyon took the jug and let the moonshine explode down his gullet; and when he saw the pleading light in Flower's eyes, he handed her the jug. She snatched it eagerly from him and managed two quick swallows before Koker was able to wrestle it out of her grasp.

Canyon got to his feet.

Koker looked at his wife. "Ain't we got plenty room for O'Grady?"

"Why, sure," she replied. Then she looked at Canyon. "You sleep in barn. Plenty room."

"I'd appreciate that," Canyon told her.

In fact, he leapt at the prospect of escaping the

cabin's oppressive confines. The good, clean, honest essence of fresh horseshit and urine stomped into moldy hay would be a welcome relief. He thanked the woman for his supper and bid them good night. Crossing the littered yard a moment later, he sucked in the high, clear mountain air with enormous relief.

Canyon's sleep was fitful and restless, punctuated with nightmares of plunging cattle and gun flashes. Abruptly he sat up, fully awake. A knife blade in Ben Koker's upraised hand glinted in the darkness above him. Canyon rolled to one side as the blade plunged down, the force of its thrust sinking the blade's tip deep into the barn's rotting floor board. Canyon grabbed Koker's wrist and twisted. The homesteader cried out, the knife dropping from his grasp. Canyon jumped to his feet and hauled Koker up after him.

With his left hand grasping Koker's right wrist, Canyon punched Koker in his midsection. His clenched fist burrowed in almost deep enough to bend the man's backbone. Gasping, Koker slammed back against the side of a stall. Canyon kept after him remorselessly. He released Koker's wrist and began punching him in the face, each blow a powerful, measured stroke. Canyon finished the flurry with a looping right that sent Koker reeling, his head snapping back against one of the barn's poles with sickening force.

Uttering a discouraged sigh, Koker slid down the length of the pole, then toppled sideways into a pile of horseshit. Canyon grabbed the man's lank hair and lifted his head. In the dim light he could see blood trickling from his right nostril. In the sudden silence Canyon heard cautious steps crossing the yard. He let Koker's head fall forward as Flower stepped cautiously into the barn's open doorway. She was having trouble seeing into the barn's lightless gloom. Held at the ready was her husband's Hawken. As she took an uncertain step into the barn, Canyon snatched up the knife Koker had dropped, grabbed Koker's hair, pulled his head back and placed the knife against Koker's neck, its sharp edge just breaking the skin. He felt Koker come awake and pull back, gasping.

"I got Ben's knife," Canyon called to Flower. "I'm holding it against his throat. Drop the rifle or I'll slit it."

She promptly laid the rifle down.

"I tell him he is crazy to do this thing."

Canyon left Ben and picked up the rifle. "You better go see to him," he told her.

She hurried past him and left the barn a moment later with her cadaverous husband in her arms. She carried him as easily as a child would a rag doll.

The next morning Flower took time out from nursing her husband to make herself and Canyon an enormous breakfast of steak, eggs, and fried potatoes, a breakfast Canyon consumed in the clear morning air on the porch. As he mounted up afterward, Flower stepped off the porch and peered up at him.

"Go in peace, mister," she said, shading her eyes.

"You want to tell me why Ben came after me?"

She shrugged her massive shoulders. "He think

maybe he trade you to Lance Caulder—for maybe two steers."

"It was a lousy idea," Canyon told her, gathering up his reins and pulling his horse around. "Lance would have shot both of us, and there'd be no free beef. Much obliged for the hospitality."

She stepped back and he rode out.

Some distance from the cabin, he glanced back. Flower was sitting on the porch in a rocker, holding the jug of moonshine in her lap and singing an Indian chant in a high, sing-song voice. Canyon was not sure whether her chant was in celebration of her deliverance from Canyon or from the vigilance of her husband who had kept her so long from the jug.

He turned back around and spurred on the palomino.

The Dixieland ranch buildings sat on a flat at the end of a long, lush pasture that reached for miles, clear to a high pass in the distance. Despite the fine quality of the pasture, as Canyon rode across it, he saw no sign of Dixieland cattle. Indeed, during the long ride down the center of the rolling pastureland, he managed to spook only a few jackrabbits. Within a half mile of the ranch buildings, Canyon moved into the timber bordering the flat and kept up the slope until he found a clear ridge above the ranch. He dismounted in the timber behind the ridge, walked to the other side of it, found a tree and slumped down, his back resting against it. Then he built a smoke, his Henry resting across his knees.

It was midafternoon and so quiet below that for

a dismal while O'Grady considered the possibility that he had arrived at an empty ranch—that Lance Caulder and his riders were in Silver Creek licking their wounds. And then the ranchhouse door opened and out onto the porch stepped Lance Caulder. Beside him was Slim Winner, the rider who had followed Canyon to Placer City. Caulder pulled the door shut, and as the two men stepped down off the porch and headed for the bunkhouse, Canyon raised his rifle, sighted, and fired.

Dirt exploded at Caulder's feet. Without looking, the two men turned and raced back to the porch, then spun about to peer in Canyon's direction, six-guns materializing in their hands. At that distance, Canyon realized, neither man could make out who he was. But they obviously saw the glint of Canyon's rifle barrel. Canyon put two quick shots into the side of the ranchhouse as the two men ducked back inside it.

Canyon bellied down beside the tree and put his sights on the door and sent two slugs through it. He saw the wood leaping as the lead punched through. He waited a moment, then put two shots through the window by the door. He shifted his sights and put another shot into the door.

The faint shout of angry, confused voices in the ranchhouse came to him. Suddenly there was a shot from the broken window, and Canyon heard the thud of the bullet in the tree trunk a few feet above his head. He smiled a little and moved behind the tree trunk, and then put two more shots through the window. He heard a bitter cursing inside the ranchhouse, settled himself comfortably onto the grass, and watched. Presently a rifle barrel poked tentatively out of the window, and Canyon put a shot at it. The barrel withdrew. Canyon put three more quick shots through the window, pulled back, reloaded the Henry, then waited.

Nothing moved below him. But Canyon was willing to wait. He had no warrant for Lance Caulder, and though not long ago the man had attempted to murder him, there was no way Canyon could bring Lance in legally. On the other hand, if Lance Caulder lost his head and came at Canyon like a wet hornet and Canyon was forced to kill him in self-defense, a crude, but effective justice would have finally prevailed. Canyon was sure the president would accept—though perhaps reluctantly—this resolution of his commitment to see to it that Lance Caulder paid for his crimes.

Abruptly a rifle opened up on Canyon from a rise beyond the ranch house. There was a third man down there after all. He must have been in the bunkhouse when Canyon opened up. The rifleman's fire was rapid and not very accurate, but Canyon could not afford to ignore it. As he picked up his Henry and ducked back into the trees, he saw Lance and Winner bolt from the ranchhouse, heading for the barn. After that stampede, these two men were all Lance had at his disposal.

Canyon reached the palomino, cinched the girth tight, and vaulted into it. He put the horse up the timbered slope, skirting behind the ranch buildings, and kept to its cover for a mile until he regained the flat. He was a good two miles across the flat, heading south, when he glanced behind him and saw the first horseman boil out of the timber in pursuit. Behind him came two others. That first horseman, Canyon knew, would be Lance Caulder. Slowing down some, he peered more closely at the other two and saw that the third rider—the rifleman who had opened up on him from behind the ranch house—was Bull Renfrew, the big logger who had worked Seth Barton over so efficiently.

Canyon waited a moment to make sure the hook was in all the way, then clapped his heels to the palomino and resumed his flight, swinging to the southwest into a patch of timber. He was grimly pleased. There were still long hours of daylight before him, and miles of open country. Lance Caulder and his two gunslicks would be furious enough to push their mounts to their limits.

Canyon now had things his way. On his tail were not one, but three angry wet hornets.

As Canyon splashed across the shallow stream and rode farther into the canyon, he realized he had passed this way before and had headed back here for that reason. He dismounted and slapped the palomino's rump smartly, sending it toward a grassy sward, partially shielded by a break in the rock wall. Then he flattened himself behind a pile of boulders and waited. His three pursuers would soon be charging after him into the canyon's mouth—and there would be nothing but an open stream between them.

Before long, he heard pounding hoofs approaching. O'Grady placed his Colt on the ground beside him, then checked the Henry's load. The three riders appeared, plunging after him recklessly, certain their numbers were sufficient to take him. Canyon tracked the closest rider, Bull Renfrew, and squeezed off a shot. Bull's horse dropped under him, spilling him forward onto the ground. Lance and Winner reined in, pulling their mounts around so sharply, the horses nearly went down. Canyon levered quickly, tracked Lance and fired. The shot missed and a second later the two riders were out of sight beyond the canyon's mouth.

Canyon splashed across the stream as Bull pushed himself up onto his hands and knees, fumbling for his hat. Leaving his hat where it was, Bull twisted his head to peer more closely at Canyon.

"Damn! It *is* you. This here is crazy. Lance said he killed you."

"Lance shouldn't brag."

Bull shook his head and peered intently at Canyon. The fall off his horse had stunned him only momentarily. "You better get out of here, mister," he told Canyon evenly. "Lance's goin' to be back here soon. This time he'll finish you."

"Get up on your feet, Bull."

Bull pushed himself erect. "I ain't got nothin' against you, mister."

"You didn't have anything against Seth Barton either, but that didn't stop you from setting him up."

"I did what I was told."

"By your keeper. Lance Caulder. Now drop your gun belt."

"Sure."

Bull's hands dropped to his belt buckle, then

paused. His eyes narrowed and his right shoulder lifted suddenly as he reached back. Almost reluctantly, Canyon flipped up his rifle and squeezed the trigger. But Bull ducked low and swept around his revolver with startling speed and knocked aside Canyon's rifle barrel. Canyon's shot went wild. Bull fired at him hastily, the slug searing past O'Grady's shoulder, its passage a hot whisper in his ear. Down on one knee, he brought up his rifle again and fired point blank at Bull's huge chest. Bull's body shuddered. The big man dropped to his knees, then pitched forward onto his face. Where his chest struck the gravelly soil, a dark stain welled into view.

Canyon walked over to Bull and was reaching down for his revolver when he heard the sound of someone jacking a fresh load into a Henry's firing chamber. Canyon left Bull and ran back toward the stream. The rifle behind him cracked and a bullet sent up a geyser of water inches from his plunging feet. When he reached the other side of the stream, he flattened himself behind the rocks on its bank and swung up his rifle, his eyes sweeping the far side of the stream. Just above the rim of a depression, he saw the rifleman's hat and then the barrel of his rifle. Canyon steadied his weapon, sighted carefully, and squeezed off a shot. The hat vanished, but the rifle remained steady. It's muzzle blazed and a bullet whanged angrily off a rockface beside Canyon.

He kept his eye peeled as he waited for the second shot and when it came from the same source, he realized that the rifleman—it had to be either Caulder or Winner—was trying to pin him down while his companion circled around Canyon to take him from the rear. Canyon waited for the rifleman's next shot. When it came, Canyon leaped to his feet, left the rocks and ran for the canyon wall behind him. As he ran, he glanced up and saw a stalking figure just gaining the rim above him. It was Slim Winner, which meant Caulder was behind Canyon. Winner swung up his rifle and fired. The ground in front of Canyon exploded, sending mean shards of rock up into his face. He kept on, reached a cleft in the cliff wall and, running into it, found a narrow game trail leading to the canyon rim. He charged up it, Winner no longer visible. In the canyon below, Lance Caulder was standing in plain sight on the other side of the stream. He lifted his rifle and sent a steady stream of fire up at Canyon. But his aim was poor, the bullets whining off the slope far below him.

Approaching the rim, Canyon kept on without checking his stride, his legs driving him steadily up the steep trail. When he reached the rim, he flung himself onto the ground, his Colt held out in front of him. Winner was ready and fired on Canyon the moment he hit the ground. Canyon was almost blinded by the muzzle flash and the stinging gravel thrown up by the bullet. His eyes closed, he fired blindly, emptying his revolver. When he opened his eyes, Slim Winner was sprawled on his back less than six feet from him.

Canyon pushed himself erect and walked over to inspect the downed man. One look told him all he needed to know. More than one bullet had slammed into Winner's heart, and both of his eyes were frozen open, staring in startled surprise up at Canyon. He had probably been dead before he hit the ground.

From the canyon floor below came Lance Caulder's shout: "O'Grady! That you up there?"

Leaving Winner, Canyon walked to the rim and looked down. Astride his mount, Caulder was peering up at him.

"It's me, all right," Canyon shouted back. "And your man's dead up here."

"Why ain't you?" Caulder yelled. "You're a hard man to kill, O'Grady!"

"You're a lousy shot, Caulder."

"Well, I ain't done with you yet."

"I'll be right down. We can settle this now."

"No. Not here. I'll be waitin' in Placer Town."

He swung his horse around and rode off, the beat of his hoofs fading swiftly. Canyon watched Caulder disappear, then glanced back at Winner. A shadow flitted across the still body. Canyon glanced up and saw a buzzard dropping lower.

He started back down the steep trail to his palomino.

10

Canyon rode into Placer Town late that night. He reckoned that Lance Caulder was at least an hour ahead of him. As he rode in, he saw empty sidewalks and empty streets. The only light came from the window in the doc's office, but the saloon was dark, despite the horses lined up at the hitch-rack in front of it. The hotel looked especially foreboding, since not a single gleam came from any of its windows.

Placer Town—and Lance Caulder—was waiting for him.

Canyon took out his Colt and rested it on his thigh—and kept on riding, a lightning rod waiting for the first quick flash. As he rode past an alley's black mouth, the door from the doc's office on the second floor opened.

"Watch out, Canyon!" the doc cried. "It's a trap!"

A man appeared on the landing beside the doc and clubbed him so hard he toppled down the stairs. Canyon heard the sickening thud as the doctor's head struck a step near the bottom. Leaping from the palomino, he snaked the Henry from its scabbard in one swift pull and with a slap on its rump sent the horse on down the street out of the line of fire. Crouching low, he made a dash for the steps, the rifle at his hips blazing up at the Dixieland rider on the landing as the man plunged back into the doc's office.

At once, a barrage opened up on Canyon from the darkened store fronts and windows behind Canyon. Too late he realized he had underestimated the manpower at Lance's disposal. Placer Town—not Silver Creek—was where the remnants of his riders had gone to lick their wounds, and they must have been waiting for Lance to join them here. Canyon pulled the unconscious doctor off the steps and ducked behind them, doing his best to return the fire. He did this without panic, aiming carefully at spots behind gun flashes. Occasionally his hot lead caused a store front's window to shiver into a thousand pieces; but his fire was rapid enough and dangerous enough to keep Lance's men at bay. Meanwhile, the open stairway made an efficient barrier to the lead hurled at him, and when the fusilade slackened, Canyon took the chance to reload his Henry.

He heard a groan, glanced down, and saw the doc's eyes flicker as he regained consciousness.

"You all right?" Canyon asked him.

"I don't think anything's broken, but my head aches."

"No reason it shouldn't, from what I saw."

"I'll be all right."

"Who's upstairs in your office?"

The doc sat up cautiously. "Two of Caulder's riders."

"What're they doin' up there?"

"Lance's been waiting for you to ride in. And

you sure didn't disappoint him any. He's spotted his riders all over town. And one of them he sent up to my office to finish off Seth Barton. But I warned Seth, so he barricaded himself in the back room."

"And left you in the office to face Caulder's man."

"Seth didn't have any choice, Canyon."

A rifle shot came from the darkened saloon across the street. The bullet bit out a chunk of the stairwell. Canyon ducked and returned fire without much hope that he had hit anyone.

"How many are out there?" Canyon asked the doc.

"Seven, maybe eight. A lot less than there used to be. Most of his riders got chewed up, I heard, when Tenny's Hatchet crew caught them with the herd they rustled."

Canyon knew all about that. "From what you just told me," he told the doc, "those two in your office are caught between Seth and me. I'm going up there. Keep your head down."

"Be careful."

At that moment one of Caulder's riders appeared from around the corner of the building, a Colt in each hand. Canyon fired at him through the steps, placing a slug in his heart. The man went down on his knees, his fingers squeezing convulsively on the triggers of his two six-guns, sending a futile charge of hot lead into the ground. Canyon used the commotion to cover him as he ducked around in front of the stairway and charged up the steps and without pause kicked open the door to the doc's office. In the light cast by a lamp sitting on the file cabinet, Canyon saw the shadowy figures of the two men crouching behind the desk. He dropped to the floor and pumping his Henry sent four quick shots under the desk, the slugs tearing into one of the men.

The other—the same man who had clubbed the doc—jumped up onto the desk and sent a round down at Canyon. The slug buried itself in the floor beside Canyon's cheek. Awkwardly, Canyon rolled onto his back and brought up the Henry, fired and missed. He was desperately jacking a new shell into the firing chamber when the door behind the desk opened and Seth Barton limped out and swung his crutch at the man on the desk, catching him on the back of the neck, smashing through the vertebrae. The man toppled off the desk, sprawling heavily, awkwardly, on the floor.

"Thanks, Seth," Canyon said, getting to his feet. "He had me dead to rights. You all right?"

"I'm fine."

"How's that hip of yours?"

"Still hurts some, but at least I ain't bedridden. Where's the doc?"

"He's down at the bottom of the steps, nursing a sore head. But he'll be all right."

As Canyon spoke, he went to the window and looked down at the street below. The moon's pale glow gave him a clear view of Lance's men flitting from store front to store front as they closed in, six-guns gleaming in their fists. He counted five men in all; and as he watched they broke from the darkened store fronts and raced across the street toward the stairwell.

"Here they come!" Canyon said, tossing Seth his Colt.

Looking back down, Canyon saw Lance Caulder step out of the saloon, a double-barreled shotgun in his hand. Canyon flung up the window.

"I got you covered, Caulder! Call off your dogs!"

The man glanced up at Canyon. "Not on your life, O'Grady!"

Caulder flung up his shotgun. Before he could fire, Canyon snapped a shot down at him. The bullet shivered a window beside him as he ducked back hastily through the batwings. His men, however, were not as intimidated and at once sent a wild, but steady fusilade up at Canyon, shattering the doctor's window. Glass shards ricocheted about the room like shrapnel. At the same time, Canyon could hear the windows in the next room shattering as they too were taken out.

Canyon and Barton dropped to their hands and knees as the bullets tore into the ceiling and walls. Plaster sifted down over them, a few bullets made a wild racket as they slammed into the doctor's file cabinet. Another ricocheting round disintegrated a bottle of whiskey sitting on a bookshelf.

"Jesus," Barton said. "We're none of us goin' to get out of this."

Canyon told Seth to keep his head low, then scuttled across the floor and slipped out onto the landing. Glancing down the steps, he saw that Doc Sanderson had vanished into the night. Lying prone on the landing, he kept his eyes on the alley's entrance and waited. The rattle of rifle fire from the street kept steady for a while, then slackened. From the saloon came Lance Caulder's voice, issuing curt orders.

"Get up them steps! Finish them off!"

Canyon was suddenly aware of Seth joining him on the landing.

"Let the bastards come," Seth muttered. "It's about time I paid them back for this bum hip."

"They're on their way."

"I'm ready."

"Don't fire until I tell you."

Seth grinned. "You want to wait until we see the whites of their eyes?"

"Something like that."

Seth cocked Canyon's pistol.

Then came the chink of spurs as Caulder's men approached the alley entrance. There was a momentary pause, some hurried whispering— then, out of the darkness and up the steps Caulder's men poured. It was a damn fool rush into the mouth of hell for those leading the charge. Canyon held his fire until the first two men were almost close enough for him to reach out and touch.

"Now!" Canyon told Seth.

He squeezed the Henry's trigger, levered, and fired again. Beside him, Seth hammered away. Canyon saw the hail storm of lead slamming into the men; the terrible, withering fire sent those in front hurtling backward upon the heads and shoulders of those racing up the stairs behind them. The carnage was sickening. The cries and screams of wounded men filled the night as they toppled back down the stairs and struck the ground, and were then buried by the wounded men tumbling onto them. Only one man prevented himself from falling back down the steps. He had caught himself and was clinging to the bannister, his drawn revolver swinging in his hand.

Canyon held his fire.

"Go on," he told the man. "Get out of here!"

Slapping his Colt back into his holster, the Dixieland rider spun about and plunged down the steps, leaped over the tangled, groaning men at the bottom and vanished into the alley. Two men on the ground who had survived the fusilade jumped to their feet and vanished into the alley. A moment later Canyon heard the pound of their horses as the surviving Dixieland riders left town.

That left only Lance Caulder.

Canyon ran down the steps and across the street. Shouldering through the saloon's batwings, he found the inside of the saloon as black as a whore's heart. He kept going and ducked behind the bar just as Lance Caulder—barricaded behind an overturned table—let loose both barrels of his shotgun. The buckshot shattered the mirror and exploded the neat pyramids of glasses on the shelves, showering broken glass down onto Canyon's hat brim. He could hear Lance slipping two more shells into his shotgun.

Lance yelled, "Stick your head up, asshole, and I'll blow it off for you. Ah won't miss this time."

Canyon snapped a shot at Caulder and heard the slug rip harmlessly into the tabletop behind which Lance was crouched. Caulder's shotgun roared back at him. The upper portion of the bar absorbed most of the buckshot and a few more splinters from the mirror showered down on Canyon. Canyon heard Caulder's deep chuckle. This was a standoff and Caulder knew it.

Abruptly, the cold muzzle of a revolver came to rest on the back of Canyon's neck. He froze. Belle's voice came soft and clear to him. She had crept down the bar in the darkness and was now crouched beside him.

"Let him out of this, Canyon."

"You mean let him ride out?"

"Yes."

"I can't do that."

Caulder recognized Belle's voice. "Belle, that you over there?" he called.

"Yes, Lance."

"You want to get your head blown off? Get out of here!"

"I'm saving your hide, Lance."

"Dammit, Belle. I got this son of a bitch dead to rights. Soon as he shows his head, I'll blow it off."

"The only thing you're blowing up is the saloon. I got him covered, Lance. Get out of town and take your gunslicks with you."

Canyon heard Lance get to his feet, chuckling. "Sure thing, Belle. Anything you say—soon's I finish off this bastard. Now, you just keep him covered until I take him off your hands."

"No, Lance."

"What do you mean, Belle?"

"I mean if you come over here, I'll shoot you."

"What's the matter with you, woman? You crazy? That son of a bitch's cut down most of my men. He's in league with them hill ranchers."

"I don't care, Lance. Go on. Do what I said. Ride out—like the rest of your hired killers."

"You mean you're standing up for this Yankee?"

"You forget, Lance. I'm a Yankee, too."

"This ain't fair, Belle."

"What's fair, Lance? Sending your men to burn out Hatchet and the Sun Ranch? Killing Helen Steadman's father? Sending your thugs across the street to kill Seth Barton?"

"You heard her, Caulder," Canyon told him. "She means it, too. Take this chance and get out of here—while you still can."

Canyon heard Lance curse, then fling down his shotgun and start for the saloon's door. Canyon got up, Belle keeping close beside him, the muzzle of her revolver still pressed against the back of his neck. As Lance neared the batwings, Belle increased the revolver's pressure to make certain that Canyon did not use his rifle. Before Caulder stepped through the batwings, he paused to look back at Canyon and Belle, visible to him now in the darkness behind the bar.

"You'll regret this, Belle!"

"Get out, Lance. Now. And leave these hills. You're too damn bull-headed to admit it, but right now I'm saving your ass."

With a bitter, scornful laugh, Caulder shouldered his way through the batwings. The muzzle's pressure on Canyon's neck decreased as Belle moved away and placed the revolver down on the bar. Canyon pushed past her and hurried around the end of the bar.

"Canyon," she called after him. "Let him go. Please!"

Reaching the batwings, Canyon peered out. Caulder was already astride his horse, calling out to those of his men who could still ride to mount up. Across the street at the mouth of the alley, Canyon glimpsed Seth Barton, gun in hand, pressed flat against the side of the building, watching Caulder warily. The doc was dimly visible in the darkness under his stairwell tending to those wounded who could still benefit from his care.

No riders answered Caulder's summons.

He waited a moment longer, then wheeled impatiently and headed out of town, quickly lifting his horse to a gallop. As he rode, he took out his revolver. His wild rebel yell suddenly filled the night as he began shooting back at the saloon. But his shots succeeded only in shivering a few more windows, and then—his rebel yell fading rapidly— he vanished into the night.

Canyon and Belle hurried across the street to join Seth and offer any assistance to the doc. It was while Belle was comforting one badly shot-up Dixieland rider that Canyon heard distant shouts, followed by a flurry of gunfire. Then came the sudden clatter of hooves. He left the doc and stepped back out into the street just in time to see Lance Caulder racing back to Placer Town on foot, a hard-riding horseman chasing him—Tenny, Hatchet's owner. Caulder turned and fired over his shoulder at Tenny, but missed. He turned back around then and tried desperately to dodge away from the onrushing horsemen; but Tenny cut him down with a single round, then circled him slowly as he carefully punched shot after shot into Caulder's prostrate figure.

"Lance! Oh, my God," breathed Belle.

She left Canyon and ran up the street to Caulder's side.

Canyon kept pace with her, but pulled back some as he approached the bullet-riddled figure, allowing Belle to drop to Caulder's side. Belle seemed beside herself as she cradled the ex-bushwhacker's head in her lap, crooning softly to him. As gently as he could, he pulled Belle back onto her feet. For a moment she clung to Canyon, her face buried in his chest, and then one of her girls hurried over and took her from him and led her away.

Tenny remained on his mount as his riders and Sam Gills charged down the street and pulled up alongside him. Then he and Gills dismounted, the rest of their riders dismounting also. Tenny took a step closer to Canyon, peering at him in some amazement.

"Damned if you ain't a sight for sore eyes, O'Grady," he said, shaking his head in wonderment. "Jim Swallows told us you was dead. He swore it. Said he saw Lance Caulder bring you down."

"Caulder came close enough, sure enough. Too damn close. I got a crease under my hatband that'll keep the memory fresh. Where is Swallows?"

"Back at the Box J, I reckon."

"Alone?"

"You mean is Helen Steadman with him?"

"I guess that's what I mean."

"She's there. Them two are goin' to get married, I hear."

Out of the darkness a few townsmen came skulking now, eyes wide in their eagerness for blood; and soon the street was filled with the murmur of excited voices as dark, jostling shapes shifted ever closer to get a glimpse of Dixieland's dead chief— Lance Caulder, the Confederate bushwhacker who had once ridden with the infamous Quantrill. The sheriff and town constable appeared then—like rats chased from a town dump. They looked uncomfortably down at Lance Caulder's sprawled body, then around at Tenny and Gills and their ring of weary, glowering riders. In a voice laced with contempt, Tenny told the two men they were not needed—then ordered them to go fetch the undertaker.

The two scurried off.

"That's all them buzzards are good for," Tenny remarked, watching them go. "If I have anything to say about it, there'll be some new elections in this town pretty damn soon."

Seth, using his crutch with great dexterity, swung out of the darkness and pulled up beside Canyon, the doc with him. Sanderson examined Caulder, then glanced up at Canyon and Seth and shook his head.

"Too bad," Seth said bitterly. "I would've preferred to have seen a rope tighten around that bastard's neck."

"Think again, Seth. Maybe it's better this way. It's over now. Like the war."

"Then we're through here?"

"Not entirely."

Tenny frowned and Sam Gills stepped closer.

"What's that, O'Grady?" Gills said. "You figure you got more business in Placer Town?"

"Nothing to concern you and Tenny. I just thought I'd ride out to the Box J and bid Swallows and Helen good-bye."

"Well now, that's right thoughtful of you," Gills said.

But the slight frown on his and Tenny's face told Canyon that both men knew there was a lot more to Canyon's visit to the Box J than Canyon was willing to admit. But neither man said a word as they turned about and swung back into their saddles and wheeled their mounts. Their riders mounted up quickly and rode after the two men. Watching them ride out of Placer Town, Canyon felt a growing sense of unease as he realized what news he would be carrying to the Box J.

And to Helen Steadman.

Biff Collins and two Box J riders met Canyon before he reached Swallows's ranchhouse, riding silently out of the tall grass to encircle him. The foreman nudged his mount close and from the look on his face, Canyon got some idea of how Lazarus must have felt when he rose from the dead.

"We thought you was dead, O'Grady," Collins said bluntly.

"I sure hope to hell you are wrong."

Collins laughed—and then his beefy face went dark with concern. "The boss must've been seeing things."

"It was a rainy night, Biff."

"That so?"

Canyon said nothing more as he let Biff and the two riders escort him into the ranch's compound and up to the hitch-rack in front of the ranchhouse. He did not dismount. Helen appeared on the porch first, and a moment later Jim Swallows stepped out beside her.

The astonishment Helen felt was obvious in her expression, but it was Swallows who spoke first.

"It's you, then, O'Grady. You're . . . alive!"

"No thanks to you."

"What the hell is that supposed to mean?"

"You say Lance Caulder shot me?"

"It was raining. I might have been mistaken."

"You're right, Swallows. It was raining. But I was not unconscious. While you and Lance Caulder sat your horses and discussed my fate, I heard every word. And when Caulder suggested you pull the trigger, I was touched by your response. We'd shared a jug on your porch, so you didn't want to do it. Later, though, you joined him in firing down at my body as it was swept along in that torrent."

"You're mad, O'Grady. You have no proof of any of this."

"That's right, Swallows. It's my word against yours. Something you ought to know. Lance Caulder is dead. And with it, any chance that you and he will be dividing up the hill ranches among yourselves and the other cattlemen on this plateau."

"Canyon O'Grady," Helen said, her voice hushed. "What . . . what are you saying? That Jim here and Lance Caulder were . . ."

"Yes. They were working together, Helen. Your father's Sun Ranch was part of it. Jim wasn't willing to wait until your father consented to your marriage. He wanted to make sure this land would be his. Caulder made sure for him."

"I don't believe it!"

"Didn't expect you would—not at first, anyway. But you came out of the night once to take me to shelter, and you and your father stood by me against Caulder. I figured I owed you this warning in return. I wish it could have been a more welcome message."

The Box J riders had come out of the bunkhouse, and along with Collins and the two riders were listening intently. They stood their ground now, looking up at Swallows in some amazement. If not every hand believed what O'Grady had just told Helen, enough did to rivet the rest. Now it was up to Swallows to give a convincing explanation.

They—and Helen—waited.

Swallows took a step to one side, away from Helen. He had been wearing his six-gun when he stepped out of the house and now he let his right hand drop to his side.

"You're a liar, O'Grady. I had nothing to do with burning out the Sun Ranch."

"What made you think I was dead?"

"Caulder. He told me he had killed you. I believed him."

"That mean you and Caulder were on talkin' terms? Good friends, were you? Partners maybe?"

"That's a lie. You can't prove it."

Helen turned about to face Swallows, her face pale. Something in Swallows's voice told her the man was lying. The Box J riders sensed the same thing. Realizing he had no way of refuting Canyon, he became desperate to stop the man's damning testimony and drew his revolver. Canyon flung himself off the palomino. As soon as he hit the ground, he rolled over, then rolled over a second time and came up shooting. His first round sent Swallows's gun flying from his shattered fist, the second one caught him in the leg, spinning him to the floor of the porch. Helen rushed to his side. With a curse, he pushed her aside and scrambled for the dropped six-gun.

Canyon raced up onto the porch and kicked the gun off it.

Staring up at Canyon, his one good hand clutching his bloody leg, Swallows swore darkly, bitterly, his face livid with rage and frustration.

In that instant, all doubts vanished. Helen and every Box J rider knew that Canyon had spoken the truth. Jim Swallows had been in league with Lance Caulder, and not only that, but he had planned to profit in the death of Helen Steadman's father. Canyon holstered his weapon, left the porch, and mounted his palomino.

"Will you wait while I saddle a horse," Helen asked.

"Of course," Canyon told her.

As she descended the porch steps, Swallows pulled himself into the ranchhouse and vanished. His men turned their backs on the house and started for the barn with Helen. Like Helen, they were leaving Jim Swallows alone with his gun shot wounds and the yawning emptiness in his soul.

Colonel Charles Cutler moved out from behind his desk to shake Canyon's hand. The grasp was warm, solid—despite the deep weariness visible in the colonel's eyes.

"The president sends his regrets, but this business with the Congress is taking all of his time, it seems. For the first time today, I heard talk of impeachment."

"Can they do that, do you think?"

"It is all talk, I am sure. But it seems nothing will appease these damned carpetbaggers. They want the South to bleed until there is nothing left."

"Did the president read my report?"

"Yes. I must admit it, he was disappointed. He would have liked to bring that bushwhacker to justice. There are many good reasons why a butcher of Caulder's reputation should be hanged publicly. Few of these carpetbaggers in Congress would dare to doubt then the president's sincere effort to punish such Confederate bandits."

"It would have been impossible to take Caulder alive."

"Your report makes that clear, and the president understands perfectly your dilemma once Seth Barton had revealed his and your presence in the area. Now tell me, the president is anxious to know if you think the Confederate sympathizers in New Mexico Territory will make trouble for the Union."

"The war is over, Colonel. They know it. Besides, I have a feeling that before long, they'll be busy with Apaches and Utes. And on my way back across Texas I saw some very angry Comanches. The aborigines are not going to take the loss of their land lightly."

The colonel sighed. "More trouble with them, you surmise?"

"Yes. And it will not be an easy task pacifying such fiercely warlike tribes."

"Perhaps not," he said with a sigh. "It looks as

if this government will have to call once more upon the services of Kit Carson. Thank you, Mr. O'Grady."

Canyon got to his feet. The colonel skirted his desk and escorted Canyon to the door. "You'll be hearing from us soon," he said, as he pulled the door open. "This country needs men of your calibre."

"Thank you, Colonel," Canyon said, stepping through the doorway, "and give my regards to the president. Tell him I wish him luck."

"He'll appreciate that."

The colonel shook Canyon's hand, then shut the door. Canyon walked down the corridor and descended the wide marble stairway. He was anxious to get far from this damp, gloomy city where little hard-eyed men did what they could to bring down a president Canyon respected deeply. A moment later, as he climbed into a hacky, the sun broke through the clouds.

Canyon hoped it was an omen, but remembering Colonel Cutler's worried eyes, he did not think it was.